MY STORY

LEICESTERSHIRE & NORTHAMPTONSHIRE

Edited by Lisa Adlam

WHERE WOULD YOU GO?

ABOUT THIS BOOK ...

First published in Great Britain in 2015 by:

 Young**Writers**

Remus House
Coltsfoot Drive
Peterborough
PE2 9BF
Telephone: 01733 890066
Website: www.youngwriters.co.uk

Printed and bound in the UK by BookPrintingUK
Website: www.bookprintinguk.com

WELCOME TO A WORLD OF IMAGINATION!

Dear Reader,

My First Story was designed for Key Stage I children as an introduction to creative writing and to promote an enjoyment of reading and writing from an early age.

The simple, fun storyboards give even the youngest and most reluctant writers the chance to become interested in literacy by giving them a framework within which to shape their ideas. Pupils could also choose to write without the storyboards, allowing older children to let their creativity flow as much as possible, encouraging the use of imagination and descriptive language.

We believe that seeing their work in print will inspire a love of reading and writing and give these young writers the confidence to develop their skills in the future.

There is nothing like the imagination of children, and this is reflected in the creativity and individuality of the stories in this anthology. I hope you'll enjoy reading their first stories as much as we have.

Jenni Bannister

Jenni Bannister
Editorial Manager

CONTENTS

EMMANUEL CHRISTIAN SCHOOL, LEICESTER

Zachary Taylor (5)..............................1
Noah Daniel Kenneth
Jeffers-Robinson (5)......................2
Bethan Wheeler (6)...........................3
Sina Efrem (7) 4

ENGLISH MARTYRS CATHOLIC PRIMARY SCHOOL, OAKHAM

Anna Barwell (6)................................5
Harvey Matthew Asher (7) 7
Joanna Sobanska (6) 8
Kyra Nettle (7)..................................9
Pitcha Robinson (6) 10
Thomas Hodgson (6)......................... 11
Annabelle Jean McDonald (6) 12
Daniel Valiente (5) 13
Morgan McDonald (7) 14
Tiffany Amito Donoher (6) 15
Melissa Barker (7) 16
Annabella Joy Iden (5) 17
Maddison Savage (6)........................ 18

GRANBY PRIMARY SCHOOL, LEICESTER

Tayla Goldsmith-Noyes (5)................ 19

JOHN WYCLIFFE PRIMARY SCHOOL, LUTTERWORTH

Khaliel Young (5)............................. 20
Elizabeth-Grace Jones (6) 21
Joshua Taylor (6) 22
Zara Chechlacz (5) 23

Libby Cottington (5)......................... 24
Charlie Rowley (6)............................ 25
Daniel Faulkner (6) 26
Michael David McCourt (6) 27
Evie Adkins (6) 28
Grace Elizabeth Jesson (6) 29
Lydia Hall (6) 30
Adam Riley Evans (5) 31
William Lord (6) 32
Pacey Barnett (6) 33
Ethan Richards (6) 34

KETTERING SCIENCE ACADEMY, KETTERING

Ruby Adams (6) 35
Kian Ashley Bremner (6) 36
Keira Wallis (6)............................... 37
Lois F. Green (5) 38
Cortez Antony (6) 39
Nell Gilbert (5) 40
Sonny-Lee Playford (6) 41
Riley Cross (5) 42
Aiden Jake Bell (5)........................... 43
Ayesha Kumra (6)............................ 44
Heather Thomson (6) 45

Reece Hunt (6)...........................46
Kyra Peck-Smith (6)........................47
Jacob Daniel Lattanzi (6).................48
Euan Brooks (6)................................49
Dermot Ayrton Skipper (6)...............50
Leigha Baxter (5).............................51
Aaliyah Melton (6)...........................52
Skye Parratt (6)...............................53
Chelsey-Mai Louise Church (6).........54
Olivia Shaw (6)................................55

NEWTON BURGOLAND PRIMARY SCHOOL, COALVILLE

Gabriel Ashcroft (6)...........................56
Julie Grace Nutting (5)......................57
Will Goodhew (5)..............................58
Jack Jago Saxty Watson (6).............59
Grace Cole (5) 60
Lucas Edwards (5)............................61
May Eliza Minderides (6)...................62
Phoebe Davies (6) 63
Olivia Frances Spencer (7) 65
Rebecca Harvey (6)..........................66
Seth Howling (6)................................67
Georgie Goodhew (7)........................68
Peter Simon-Strong Burton (6).........69
Oscar Jason Minderides (6) 70
George James-Strong Burton (6).....71

Jonty Norman (6)..............................72
Amber Dilkes (7)...............................73
Billy Hart (6)......................................74
Lily-Rose Robinson-Smith (6)...........75
Jimmy Aldridge (7)............................76

OLD DALBY CE PRIMARY SCHOOL, MELTON MOWBRAY

Freya Gant...77
Melissa Louise Hatley (7)...................78
Olivia Stafford (4) 79
Jorji Klein Leavis (6)..........................80
Noah Klein Leavis (6) 81

PARKLANDS PRIMARY SCHOOL, NORTHAMPTON

Matheus Rufus (6) 82
Sonny Lawrence (6) 83
Joe Cuming (7) 84
Izzy Earl (7)..85
Lola Skipworth (6) 86
Daisy Burrell (6) 87
Reece Corless (7) 88
Adam Kherry (7) 89
Knojah Kogulavarathan (7)................90
Jasmine Loasby-Cook (7)...................91
Vincent Rose (7) 92
Isabella Doherty (7)...........................93
Taylor Skates (6)...............................94
Abby Wade (7)....................................95
Oscar Morrison (6)............................96
Tamika Matika (6)..............................97
Aleena Jiji (6)......................................98
Molly Reed (7)....................................99
Megan Underwood (6).....................100
Salvatore Rendina (7) 101
Reginald Nathan Majwega (7) 103

Joshua Watts (6) 104
Evan Wilkins (6) 105
Ella May Lee (6) 106
Igor Zylka (6) 107
John-Paul Mead (6) 108
Federica Meninno-Symons (6) 109
Isabel Florence Clark (6) 110
Bertie Booth 111
Harry Coombs 112

PATTISHALL CE PRIMARY SCHOOL, TOWCESTER

Sam Broadbent (6) 113
Jack Gardner (7) 114
Nadia Ribeiro (6) 115
Sienna Ashleigh Richardson (7) 116
Alfie Newnham (7) 117
Harry Alsworth (7) 119
Ruby Louise Collins (6) 120
Seren Powell (6) 121
Piper Mullen (7) 122
Tyler Riley (7) 123
George Brand (7) 124
Rosie Burt (7) 125
Charlie Mills (7) 126
Isabella May Notridge (7) 127
Freddie Patterson-Smith (6) 128

QUEEN ELEANOR PRIMARY SCHOOL, NORTHAMPTON

Kaidi-Lei Sheehan (6) 129
Muneeb Ur Rehman (6) 130
Nikita Jerofejevs (6) 131
Manuel Gyan (5) 132
Alyssa Brannigan (6) 133
Sameeha Rahman (5) 134
Zofia Darocha (5) 135

Jai-Jai Weir (5) 136
Liam Turvey (5) 137
Thomas Hopper (5) 138
Stas Uzors (6) 139
Scarlotte Rose Wilson-Pickering (5) 140
Elton Rama (5) 141
Mason Webb (6) 142
Hubert Pietrzak (5) 143
Chanecia Morgan (6) 144
Jabed Ali (6) 145
Millie Draine (7) 146
Meja Andriukevieule (6) 147
Amber Lineham (7) 148
Mysha Ahmad (7) 149
Max Snow (7) 150

RED HILL FIELD PRIMARY SCHOOL, LEICESTER

Matthew Yates (7) 151
Owen Grassby (6) 152
Ethan Maisto (6) 153
Poppie Hoseason (6) 154
Spencer Phillips (6) 155
Aaron Chen (6) 156
Stan English (5) 157
Emily Barr (7) 158
Fatima Sanyang (7) 159
Emile Vernon (6) 160
Owain Rafferty (5) 161

Finley Gamble (7) 162
Francesca Victoria Bowen (7) 163
Joshua Michael Hall (5) 164
Shriya Kaur Suwali (6) 165
Olivia Jacques (7) 166
Scarlett Tucker (7) 167
Mark Nash (5) 168
Oliver Dunk (6) 169
Tia Bell (6) 170
Ethan Potter (6) 171
Daisie Tompsett (6) 172
Om Chauhan (6) 173
William Priestley (6) 174
Zara Sura-Roberts (6) 175
Chloe Melissa Trown (7) 176
Poppy Jasper (7) 177

St Mary's CE Primary School, Hinckley

James Hooson (6) 178
Freya Joanne Packer (6) 179
Lilly Anne Dunmore (6) 181
Stanley Smith (7) 182
Daniel Leather (6) 183
Madison Wilcox (7) 185
Rose Forrest (6) 187
Alfie Storer (7) 188
Aimee Fraser (5) 189
Lucy Edlin-Gill (6) 191
Stanley Neale (7) 192
Lacey-Ava Simmons (5) 193
Suki Chen (5) 194
Calum Thomas Dawkins (5) 195
Luis Ashby (6) 196

Kai Ryan-Evans (6) 197
Harvey Lee (6) 199

Thringstone Primary School, Coalville

Olivia Stokes (6) 200
Angel Findley (6) 201
Callum Smith (6) 202
Edith Watson (6) 203
Macie Ann Louise Shephard (6) 204
Oliver Mulheron (6) 205
Oliver Blake (5) 206
Max Johnson (6) 207
Edie Hutchinson (5) 208
William Chester (5) 209
Kai Gohil (6) 210
Oliver Peden (6) 211

Uplands Infant School, Leicester

Zoya Soneji (7) 212
Sarah Mahmoudi (7) 213
Maryam Anis (7) 214
Sanaa Jogee (7) 215
Rayhaan Mushtaq Shaikh (7) 216
Muhammad Jet (6) 217
Ricards Skaburskis (7) 218
Thafeem Cabbo (7) 219
Aaisha Sidat 220
Muhsin Meeahkhan (7) 221
Zainab Master (7) 222
Looay Jouhari (6) 223
Sairah Bhayat (6) 224
Asbah Daud (6) 225

Mohammed Rayhaan Panjwani (6) 226
Kareema Khalifa (6) 227
Kaseera Khan (6) 228
Zahra Rinde (6) 229
Jagrut Mohan (7) 230

WEEDON BEC PRIMARY SCHOOL, NORTHAMPTON

Amelia Ayers (5) 231
Siobhan Lavery (6) 232
Lori Johnson (5) 233
Laura Gurney (5) 234
Rebecca Georgina Merrey (6) 235

IMAGINE ...

Children were shown an image featuring
a magical talking book asking the question,
'Where would you like to go on an adventure?'

The children then imagined their adventures
choosing from one of five storyboards,
using the pictures and their imagination to
complete the tale – and here are the results!

JUNGLE STORY

Storyboard 1

SPACE STORY

Storyboard 2

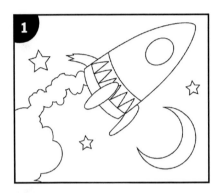

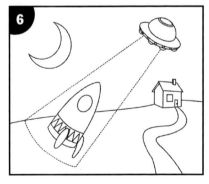

MAGICAL STORY

Storyboard 3

UNDER THE SEA STORY

Storyboard 4

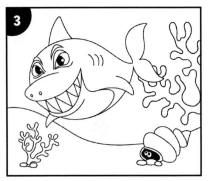

DINOSAUR STORY

Storyboard 5

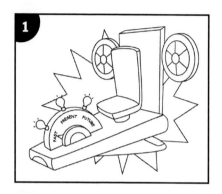

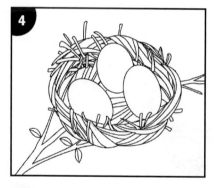

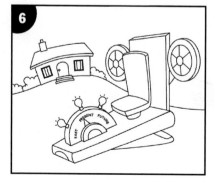

THE STORIES

ZAC'S DINOSAUR STORY

Once upon a time, there was a time machine.
There was a dinosaur who was looking for friends. He found a friend.
She laid some eggs.
The mum was coming and they hatched as she kept them warm.
They went back home.

ZACHARY TAYLOR (5)
EMMANUEL CHRISTIAN SCHOOL, LEICESTER

NOAH'S JUNGLE STORY

Once upon a time, there was a scary jungle.
In the jungle lived a rattlesnake.
The rattlesnake was scary because he had fangs.
The lion pounced.
He chased the other lions away home.
He went back home.

NOAH DANIEL KENNETH JEFFERS-ROBINSON (5)

EMMANUEL CHRISTIAN SCHOOL, LEICESTER

UNTITLED

Once upon a time, there was a girl called Sophie. She was very poor. But she was a Christian. She prayed to God every day. She prayed she would be adopted and she would have a lovely house.

One day, an old woman saw her sitting on the road. She said to her, 'Would you like it if I adopted you?'

'Yes please,' said Sophie.

They went to the place where people adopted people. They went there and they said the woman would adopt the girl. They went to the old woman's house. The woman didn't know Jesus so Sophie told her about Jesus.

It changed the woman's life. They all lived happily ever after.

BETHAN WHEELER (6)
EMMANUEL CHRISTIAN SCHOOL, LEICESTER

UNTITLED

Once there was a girl. She was playing in the playground and she saw a box. She opened the box and in the box was a rabbit. The girl took the rabbit to her home to show her mum and dad. She asked her mum and dad if she could keep the rabbit. Her mum and dad said yes and she played with her rabbit.

One day, her mum and dad made a surprise for her and for the rabbit. It was the girl's birthday party and all her friends came to her home. She was seven years old. Her rabbit was a very happy rabbit.

SINA EFREM (7)
EMMANUEL CHRISTIAN SCHOOL, LEICESTER

ANNA'S UNDER THE SEA STORY

One day, I went on a boat to go fishing. It was very windy and the boat kept wobbling. Then it turned upside down and I fell into the water.

I opened my eyes then I looked down and saw... lots of animals – crabs, shells, seaweed, jellyfish and different coloured fish.

I swam down to look closer and my eyes opened wide. In front of me was a big wooden box. I looked into the box and saw lots of treasure! Then I saw a big bad shark and then I hid in the box.

The shark saw me and chased me back to my boat. I was safe!

ANNA BARWELL (6)
ENGLISH MARTYRS CATHOLIC
PRIMARY SCHOOL, OAKHAM

HARVEY'S MAGICAL STORY

Once upon a time, there was a beautiful castle in the middle of the woods, and in the castle there lived a gorgeous princess who wore golden earrings and who had a dog called Murrey.

One day, the princess was looking out of her castle window and as she was looking up towards the bright blue sky, out of nowhere a fierce dragon appeared. He didn't look like a very nice dragon and the dragon scared the princess.

The dragon started to get restless and wondered who lived in the castle. He noticed a lady looking out of the window and thought he would scare her by breathing fire.

The dragon started wandering around looking for someone else to scare. Out of nowhere a unicorn appeared and stopped the dragon in his tracks.

The unicorn didn't seem to be scared of the dragon at all. All of a sudden, there was a great gust of wind and the unicorn disappeared in a puff of smoke and in its place stood the most scary witch holding her broomstick.

The dragon was very frightened. The witch's broomstick was actually a magic broomstick. She waved it in the dragon's face and with a 1, 2, 3, the dragon disappeared. The princess waved and smiled and the witch took herself off home. A good deed done!

HARVEY MATTHEW ASHER (7)
ENGLISH MARTYRS CATHOLIC
PRIMARY SCHOOL, OAKHAM

Joanna's Under the Sea Story

One day, I went on a boat and sailed to the deep, dark, spooky, black, slimy, gloomy water.

In the spooky sea was a crab called Elmo and some little fishes. The fishes were cute, tiny and beautiful. I found there also two bigger fishes which I called Asy and Katy.

In the afternoon a shark came to eat some things. Near the shark was scared Elmo, he hid well in his shell.

Then the shark went off to eat the mermaid who was called Chilly. Suddenly, Bubbles came and rescued Chilly and the shark was never seen again.

They had lots of fun making up a word called 'party'. So they had a party!

Finally, they went up and said goodbye, it was a lovely time.

Joanna Sobanska (6)

English Martyrs Catholic
Primary School, Oakham

KYRA'S UNDER THE SEA STORY

Once upon a time, there was a boat which was sailing on its own. Anyway, under the ocean was a crab watching some fish. He wasn't sad, he was happy and he had one friend called Ariel.

Then a hungry shark came. He was waiting to have a big giant feast. He looked around and saw Ariel... Ariel thought that he was going to be friends with her.

But her dad already knew what the shark was trying to do. And he took out his magic stick and chased the mean, greedy shark away. Ariel waved slowly and her face was very confused when the shark swam away.

But her dad told her all about what the shark was trying to do to her. Ariel was shocked at what her dad was explaining to her. But they danced and jiggled happily.

Then they went to the top of the ocean and waved goodbye to the plain boat with no one in it, which was really strange.

KYRA NETTLE (7)
ENGLISH MARTYRS CATHOLIC
PRIMARY SCHOOL, OAKHAM

PITCHA'S MAGICAL STORY

I walked on the rainbow then I saw the castle, oh, I saw something in there.

Wow! It was a dragon. What could I do?

The dragon had red eyes and it was fighting with someone.

It tried to kill the unicorn. Oh look, the dragon flew away because someone came to help the unicorn.

Yes, it was the witch. I was very happy because the unicorn was safe.

The witch was very kind and she let me have a magic broomstick to fly back home.

Then I heard someone calling me, 'Wake up, Pitcha, time to go to school.'

PITCHA ROBINSON (6)

ENGLISH MARTYRS CATHOLIC
PRIMARY SCHOOL, OAKHAM

THOMAS' JUNGLE STORY

There was a very dark wood. Some trees were thin and some were fat.

There was a snake in the forest. He was called Mr Blast Off.

The lion disturbed Mr Blast Off. He was angry. He said, 'Hsssss!'

The lion was scared.

The lion ran away. He ran all the way back to his den.

The lion saw a cottage. He thought he would be safe in the cottage.

The snake went back to bed.

THOMAS HODGSON (6)

ENGLISH MARTYRS CATHOLIC
PRIMARY SCHOOL, OAKHAM

ANNABELLE'S UNDER THE SEA STORY

I would like to go on a boat on the sea and swim with the fishes underwater and maybe become a mermaid.
I saw a shark and it frightened me so I called for my dad.
All of my friends helped scare the shark away.
We had a bubble party under the sea.
My friends I met under the sea were waving goodbye to me.

ANNABELLE JEAN McDONALD (6)
ENGLISH MARTYRS CATHOLIC
PRIMARY SCHOOL, OAKHAM

DANIEL'S MAGICAL STORY

Once upon a time, I went on an adventure to a castle. There was a gigantic rainbow.

And then I heard a roar and I saw... an enormous dragon! It was fiery and hot.

It was angry so it roared out fire! I was scared.

Then a unicorn came and scared the dragon away.

Next a witch came on her broomstick, she was a good witch.

Me and my mummy got lost on our adventure and the witch and her broomstick showed us the way home.

DANIEL VALIENTE (5)

ENGLISH MARTYRS CATHOLIC
PRIMARY SCHOOL, OAKHAM

13

MORGAN'S MAGICAL STORY

Once upon a time, there lived a wizard. The wizard lived in a magic castle. It became magic only when the rainbow came out. The colours of the rainbow were beautiful.

One day, a dragon came along. The dragon was fierce and angry, he went to the castle to burn it down.

So the dragon blew fire, and more fire until the castle burnt down.

A unicorn came over the rainbow to stop the dragon, but it was too late, the castle was gone forever.

The dragon turned into a witch and then turned the unicorn into a broomstick. The witch said, 'Go to my hut and clean it up!'

The broomstick smiled and said, 'OK you wicked witch!' So the little broomstick swept his way home!

MORGAN McDONALD (7)
ENGLISH MARTYRS CATHOLIC
PRIMARY SCHOOL, OAKHAM

TIFFANY'S MAGICAL STORY

One magical day in a castle, lived a beautiful unicorn coloured pink, blue and purple, it was very, very powerful.

A fierce dragon came with fire coming out of his mouth, he had two powerful wings.

He was very grumpy.

He growled at the kind unicorn.

The kind witch and her wand stopped the dragon by whizzing her wand.

The magic wand was happy and went home.

TIFFANY AMITO DONOHER (6)

ENGLISH MARTYRS CATHOLIC
PRIMARY SCHOOL, OAKHAM

15

MELISSA'S MAGICAL STORY

Once upon a time, there was a pretty-looking castle. It had flags on its towers that flew like kites. It was home to a princess.

A fire-breathing dragon guarded it. It was as red as blood and had claws as big as knives.

One day, the dragon breathed its mighty breath. Fire came out as fast as a fireball.

A unicorn appeared in the fire. The dragon stared at the unicorn in disbelief. It was a princess who had been turned into a unicorn by a sneaky witch.

The sneaky witch told her broomstick to go to her house in the distance to get her spell book because she wanted to find a fantastic spell.

She wanted the dragon to disappear so she could have the princess unicorn all to herself and her magic.

MELISSA BARKER (7)
ENGLISH MARTYRS CATHOLIC
PRIMARY SCHOOL, OAKHAM

ANNABELLA'S UNDER THE SEA STORY

Once upon a time, there was a father and a mermaid and there were twelve sisters.

The sisters were all colourful fish.

One day, an angry shark scared the mermaid.

He did not mean to...

He was a friendly shark.

At the end they all played together.

ANNABELLA JOY IDEN (5)

ENGLISH MARTYRS CATHOLIC
PRIMARY SCHOOL, OAKHAM

MADDISON'S UNDER THE SEA STORY

Once upon a time in the deep blue sea, there was a boat with no one in it... then some fish saw the boat. The next day, the fish was scared and the other fish and the crabs too.

Then loads of rocks were falling down and all of the fish and the crabs were hiding in their house.

A shark came to have some fish... then he swam to the fish's house... He had a big bad grin on his face.

Then a mermaid came and scared the shark away. Her dad came to bring her home. Then they had a party with loads of crabs and seahorses.

They danced all night long. Then everyone wriggled their tails and the crabs clattered their claws.

Then the mermaid and the merman saw the boat.

MADDISON SAVAGE (6)
ENGLISH MARTYRS CATHOLIC
PRIMARY SCHOOL, OAKHAM

TAYLA'S DINOSAUR STORY

Once upon a time, the machine took two people to the time of the dinosaurs.

So the two girls saw lots of dinosaurs and one said, 'I love this!'

A dinosaur ran through the forest and found a nest because he was running so fast.

Next he looked at the nest and saw the eggs were hatching.

Then the dinosaur saw another dinosaur and it was coming straight for him. The other dinosaur said, 'Go away from my eggs!'

After that, a time machine took the two girls back.

TAYLA GOLDSMITH-NOYES (5)
GRANBY PRIMARY SCHOOL, LEICESTER

KHALIEL'S SPACE STORY

One dark day, the astronaut blasted off. He saw an alien. The astronaut quickly flew away but the alien followed him. They went around and around.

The alien ran out of petrol. So he took his spaceship then he went to his mummy. He said to his mum the human was being mean.

'I'll take care of the human. Get in the alien spaceship now,' said the mad mummy.

The alien squashed the astronaut's home.

KHALIEL YOUNG (5)
JOHN WYCLIFFE PRIMARY SCHOOL, LUTTERWORTH

ELIZABETH'S UNDER THE SEA STORY

One cloudy day, there was a boat on the water.
I fell out of the boat. I saw a clownfish, a crab, even a little fish!
The shark came along in the water.
The shark was scared by the little mermaid.
They danced all together. I loved to dance!
The little mermaid and the king waved goodbye.

ELIZABETH-GRACE JONES (6)
JOHN WYCLIFFE PRIMARY SCHOOL, LUTTERWORTH

JOSHUA'S DINOSAUR STORY

One sunny day, Spacey made a time machine.

He made the time machine go to a hot place where dinosaurs lived.

A red and black T-rex came.

He saw three eggs in a nest and the T-rex was just about to take the eggs.

Suddenly, a pterodactyl came and swooped and grabbed the eggs.

Spacey ran as quick as he could into the time machine. He made it go back home and he told his mum.

JOSHUA TAYLOR (6)

JOHN WYCLIFFE PRIMARY SCHOOL, LUTTERWORTH

ZARA'S SPACE STORY

One dark night, a spaceship blasted off at night.
Next it crashed on the moon.
Then the astronaut wondered what it was.
After that an alien jumped out and said, 'Boo!'
Then the saucer lifted the astronauts.
Then the saucer took him home and he was safe.

ZARA CHECHLACZ (5)

JOHN WYCLIFFE PRIMARY SCHOOL, LUTTERWORTH

LIBBY'S DINOSAUR STORY

One stormy day, Ben made a time machine, it was gold.

There were two dinosaurs, one was spotty and one was spiky.

A T-rex came and it had very sharp teeth, it had blue eyes and green skin.

Then a nest had three eggs inside.

A giant pterodactyl came to the nest with the eggs inside and flew to get them.

Finally Ben came home with his magic time machine.

LIBBY COTTINGTON (5)

JOHN WYCLIFFE PRIMARY SCHOOL, LUTTERWORTH

CHARLIE'S UNDER THE SEA STORY

One cloudy day, a boat sat on the sea with me in it. It started to wobble and I accidentally fell out of my boat.

Then I saw all of the fish then the fish stopped and looked at me.

Next, a shark swam along and saw the crab and swam towards it.

Then a mermaid swam in front of the crab. The shark scared off the mermaid so it swam away.

The mermaid king and princess danced in the sea.

Finally, I climbed back in my boat then the mermaids waved at me.

CHARLIE ROWLEY (6)

JOHN WYCLIFFE PRIMARY SCHOOL, LUTTERWORTH

DANIEL'S SPACE STORY

One night, a man flew into space in his rocket.

Then the rocket crashed on the moon and he saw the Earth.

Next, the alien zoomed into space and the alien looked down at the moon.

Afterwards, the alien landed on the moon and said, 'Hi,' and he came out of his ship.

Then the alien sucked up the rocket to his ship.

Finally, the flying saucer brought the man home.

DANIEL FAULKNER (6)

JOHN WYCLIFFE PRIMARY SCHOOL, LUTTERWORTH

MICHAEL'S SPACE STORY

One day, the astronaut went for a fly in his rocket.

He crashed on the moon.

Next, the alien came.

He popped out of his ship. He was a green alien.

The rocket went up.

The alien helped the astronaut to get home.

MICHAEL DAVID McCOURT (6)

JOHN WYCLIFFE PRIMARY SCHOOL, LUTTERWORTH

Evie's Under The Sea Story

One cloudy day, there was a boat sailing across the blue sea.
Then I fell into the blue water and I saw a hard crab under the sea.
Then the grey shark came. He had sharp and pointy teeth.
Then the mermaid came and the shark frightened the pink mermaid.
Next, the king mermaid came and played with the pink mermaid and
they danced in the blue water all day. Then I saw my boat and climbed
in.

Evie Adkins (6)
John Wycliffe Primary School, Lutterworth

28

GRACE'S SPACE STORY

One dark night, the aliens went for a ride on the rocket. It blasted off to space. It landed on the shiny moon.

The aliens' planet went to space. They saw all of space and the sky! Next, the alien jumped out and shouted, 'Boo!' and he looked out the window.

The rocket stood still and the planet moved and they went right back home.

Finally they went to the house and watched the TV and had a roast dinner.

GRACE ELIZABETH JESSON (6)
JOHN WYCLIFFE PRIMARY SCHOOL, LUTTERWORTH

Lydia's Under The Sea Story

One windy day, I fell off my boat.
Next, the crab came along and he was smiling at the fish.
Then the scary shark came along and he scared the crab.
Next the mermaid came along and she scared the shark.
Then the king mermaid and the crab came to dance.
Lastly they danced in the water with their hands and their legs.

Lydia Hall (6)
John Wycliffe Primary School, Lutterworth

ADAM'S UNDER THE SEA STORY

One day, a boat was sitting on the water. A shark jumped up and bit my boat and then the boat wobbled and I fell out. I saw a crab.

The shark came. He scared the crab away.

There were two mermaids. They scared the shark away.

The two mermaids danced with me.

I climbed in my boat and rowed home in my boat.

ADAM RILEY EVANS (5)

JOHN WYCLIFFE PRIMARY SCHOOL, LUTTERWORTH

WILLIAM'S SPACE STORY

One night, the astronaut went to space.
Then the rocket crashed on the brown moon, oh no!
Next, the alien's rocket came!
The alien peeked out.
The alien's rocket picked the man's rocket up.
The rocket got home, hooray!

WILLIAM LORD (6)

JOHN WYCLIFFE PRIMARY SCHOOL, LUTTERWORTH

PACEY'S DINOSAUR STORY

One sunny day, Luke made a big time machine.

Luke landed on a diplodocus.

Then a T-rex saw a herbivore. The T-rex chased them. The herbivores ran away.

Then the T-rex saw two eggs. The T-rex went to get the two eggs. Suddenly, a pterodactyl swooped down and got the eggs.

PACEY BARNETT (6)

JOHN WYCLIFFE PRIMARY SCHOOL, LUTTERWORTH

ETHAN'S SPACE STORY

One very dark, gloomy day I went in my black and red rocket. I zoomed into space.

Then I bumped on a rock. The rocket was stuck on the rock.

Next there was a black, red and purple alien space rocket.

After that a green alien came to the moon.

The alien helped my rocket with me in the rocket.

I came home at last.

ETHAN RICHARDS (6)

JOHN WYCLIFFE PRIMARY SCHOOL, LUTTERWORTH

RUBY'S DINOSAUR STORY

Once I found a time machine in a chocolate factory and then I sat on the chair and looked at all of the buttons. It looked powerful and cool. Then I found a place with happy dinosaurs near a volcano. One dinosaur had a long neck and one had spikes.

There was a T-rex, he looked dangerous and his teeth were sharp and scary. The T-rex was evil and no one could defeat him.

I found some eggs in a branch, they were in a nest. They weren't hatching yet. We wanted to see the baby dinosaurs.

The flying dinosaur was rude and chasing after us and he looked mad. The dinosaur was up near the clouds.

Finally I got home for my tea, it was a very good adventure. The time machine was safe. I got back safely.

RUBY ADAMS (6)
KETTERING SCIENCE ACADEMY, KETTERING

KIAN'S DINOSAUR STORY

A long time ago, when I was in my time machine I went to a land of dinosaurs.

In the land of dinosaurs there were dinosaurs around the land.

I was going to be chased by a T-rex but I hid underground.

And when the T-rex was gone I stole all of the eggs.

A bird chased me because I stole all of the eggs.

I went home to rest for a bit.

KIAN ASHLEY BREMNER (6)

KETTERING SCIENCE ACADEMY, KETTERING

KEIRA'S DINOSAUR STORY

One time my friend invented a time machine and asked me to come on it.

The dinosaurs looked very happy at the time. They were next to a volcano pouring out lava.

The T-rex chased us, we got lost.

We found a couple of eggs.

The T-rex was happy, they found the baby eggs. They were safe. The T-rex looked inside, there was a baby inside. We went home.

We left the machine outside. We ran into our houses and sat down in our bedroom and played. It was a lot of fun, I had a lot of fun.

KEIRA WALLIS (6)
KETTERING SCIENCE ACADEMY, KETTERING

LOIS' DINOSAUR STORY

A long time ago, my friend Alice was an inventor and she built an invention, it was a time machine. We went in the time machine.
The dinosaurs were dressed up but still were people.
The T-rex chased us, we hid in the bushes. We managed to get away.
We found three golden eggs.
Mummy Dinosaur took Alice and I tried to get Alice.
We walked home.

LOIS F. GREEN (5)
KETTERING SCIENCE ACADEMY, KETTERING

CORTEZ'S DINOSAUR STORY

Once my friend said, 'Come on, let's go to my time machine.'
We went to a dinosaur world then a dinosaur chased us.
Then we got an egg.
A dinosaur chased us again then we went home.

CORTEZ ANTONY (6)
KETTERING SCIENCE ACADEMY, KETTERING

NELL'S DINOSAUR STORY

A long time ago, me and Alice went in my room and went to Dinosaur Land.

Suddenly a dinosaur came, we ran and ran. Skye came magically. I said, 'Run, run!' so that is what we did.

A T-rex ran after us, but we lost him.

We saw eggs, we thought it was a bit of a loaf of bread.

A mummy dinosaur came. We said, 'Sorry.' She made friends with us.

And *poof!* We were back home for dinner.

NELL GILBERT (5)

KETTERING SCIENCE ACADEMY, KETTERING

SONNY-LEE'S
DINOSAUR STORY

Once upon a time, my friend Euan made a lime machine.
Then we appeared in the land of dinosaurs. They were nice ones.
But then a T-rex came. We ran 300 miles.
We hid in a tree. We found some eggs. They were orange eggs.
But the mummy dinosaur came, it was fierce and scary. We ran a long
way to get to the time machine.
But we got home and there were no dinosaurs.

SONNY-LEE PLAYFORD (6)
KETTERING SCIENCE ACADEMY, KETTERING

RILEY'S DINOSAUR STORY

A long time ago, I saw Aiden. He told me Euan had made a time machine.

Me, Aiden and Euan went to the nice dinosaurs.

Then we were chased by a T-rex and I was scared.

Me, Aiden and Euan found three dinosaur eggs. They were awesome.

The mummy dinosaur chased us. We ran to the time machine and we flew home. Then we were home.

RILEY CROSS (5)
KETTERING SCIENCE ACADEMY, KETTERING

AIDEN'S DINOSAUR STORY

My friend Euan invented a machine. Then we went off.
We were back in time. There we were.
The T-rex ran after us. We ran and ran.
We found eggs in the bush. They were little eggs.
The mum chased us. We ran and ran. It was too fast.
We got in our time machine. There we were, back in time for lunch.

AIDEN JAKE BELL (5)
KETTERING SCIENCE ACADEMY, KETTERING

AYESHA'S DINOSAUR STORY

One day, I went to my time machine. I had an adventure to the dinosaurs and I was shocked, the dinosaurs were massive.

I went to the T-rex. I saw the T-rex. I quickly hid.

We went to the car to hide then I saw eggs. We took one.

The mummy bird came and chased after us. We went back to the time machine and pressed the button. When we pressed the button we had tea.

AYESHA KUMRA (6)

KETTERING SCIENCE ACADEMY, KETTERING

HEATHER'S DINOSAUR STORY

One day, I went to see my friend Euan and Euan said, 'Come and see this.'
I went to the dinosaurs and I made new friends.
A T-rex came and he was my friend.
He showed me some eggs and the eggs were gold.
His mum came and said, 'Time for bed.'
I went home too.

HEATHER THOMSON (6)
KETTERING SCIENCE ACADEMY, KETTERING

REECE'S DINOSAUR STORY

One day, me and my friend went on an adventure to the land of dinosaurs.

We saw lots of them.

We got spotted by a T-rex. We hid for a minute.

We saw three eggs in a nest. We picked one up. It was on a tree branch.

We got spotted again by a pterodactyl. It came for us.

We ran to our time machine. We got in it. We pressed the button. Just back before it could get us!

REECE HUNT (6)
KETTERING SCIENCE ACADEMY, KETTERING

KYRA'S DINOSAUR STORY

Once upon a time, there was a time-travelling machine. Euan was clever, he clicked it, he brought me. *Whoosh!* We were there!

We saw some dinosaurs that were good and they were positive. Suddenly, one of the dinosaurs came running up and me and Euan went to hide.

Euan picked up an egg and ran and ran. We had to run lots, it was quite tiring.

Another dinosaur chased. She was trying to breathe fire. Euan dropped the egg.

Finally I said, 'We are home, perfect!'

KYRA PECK-SMITH (6)
KETTERING SCIENCE ACADEMY, KETTERING

JACOB'S DINOSAUR STORY

One day, my friend Euan built a time machine. He said, 'Let's go in.
Look, there's a dinosaur.'
A T-rex started chasing us. We were scared.
Then we hid. 'Oh look, there are eggs.' We took an egg.
But then the mother came. 'Oh no!'
'Let's run home, back to have tea.'

JACOB DANIEL LATTANZI (6)
KETTERING SCIENCE ACADEMY, KETTERING

EUAN'S DINOSAUR STORY

One day, I invited Aidan and Dermot to see my time machine so I told them to hop on.

Then, *zoom!* We found a place which was called Dino World.

We looked behind us and me, Aidan and Dermot all were shaking. We were looking for hiding places because a big T-rex had come.

We found a tree, we climbed up the tree.

I said, 'Look at the eggs,' and we took the eggs. We were being chased by a pterodactyl and I told the others to hop onto the time machine to get back home for tea.

EUAN BROOKS (6)
KETTERING SCIENCE ACADEMY, KETTERING

DERMOT'S DINOSAUR STORY

One day, me and Aiden made a time machine and we got in it and Aiden pressed 'past'.

Then we travelled to the land of dinosaurs. We heard a sound.

It was a T-rex. We ran to a bush, we were scared, it was cold.

Then we saw spotty red and blue eggs in the leafy nest.

Then the mum dinosaur chased us. We ran very fast to the time machine.

Then we went home in time for dinner and we were safe.

DERMOT AYRTON SKIPPER (6)

KETTERING SCIENCE ACADEMY, KETTERING

LEIGHA'S DINOSAUR STORY

One day, Chelsey made a time machine. She let me in with her.
We went to the dinosaurs.
When we were there a T-rex chased us. 'You stop that!'
'Sorry,' he said.
'It's alright.'
'They are just eggs,' said Chelsey.
I said, 'They are nice.'
'What are you doing here?' said the mummy dinosaur.
'Getting these eggs.'
'No you aren't.'
'Let's go home.'
'OK,' said Chelsey.
Poof! We were gone.
'I am happy we are back.'

LEIGHA BAXTER (5)
KETTERING SCIENCE ACADEMY, KETTERING

AALIYAH'S DINOSAUR STORY

One sunny day, I went to an inventor. I time-travelled to a land of dinosaurs.

There were lots of dinosaurs in the land. The dinosaurs were friendly and the dinosaurs liked people.

Then a nasty T-rex came along and roared at me. It scared me so much. It chased me a lot. He chased me for a minute.

Then I saw some eggs and they looked really cute and they looked special. One of the eggs began to hatch.

Then the mother dinosaur came and screeched at me. She made me scream. So I ran with her eggs.

I got home in time because the dinosaur chased me.

AALIYAH MELTON (6)
KETTERING SCIENCE ACADEMY, KETTERING

SKYE'S DINOSAUR STORY

On Friday, Khushneet said, 'Come and see me.' She'd made a time machine. Then we saw some happy dinosaurs.

Then there was a T-rex and we ran away.

The flying dinosaur left some eggs in its nest.

Then the mummy bird came to check the eggs and see if someone had come and taken one.

Then we went home and we were in time for dinner.

SKYE PARRATT (6)
KETTERING SCIENCE ACADEMY, KETTERING

CHELSEY'S DINOSAUR STORY

Once upon a time, there was a boy called Jackson. He built a time machine. We went to see the land of dinosaurs.

There was an angry T-rex and he chased us and he was angry, super angry.

We found eggs and I was happy and brave.

A mummy bird was angry at us.

My mummy shouted, 'Chelsey and Jackson!'

We went in our machine and we went home just in time for tea.

CHELSEY-MAI LOUISE CHURCH (6)

KETTERING SCIENCE ACADEMY, KETTERING

OLIVIA'S DINOSAUR STORY

One sunny evening, I went to see my friend, Sonny, he was an inventor. He had a time machine.

We went to a dinosaur land, the dinosaurs were friendly. When we got there they were lovely but a T-rex appeared, he looked horrible. He chased me and Sonny. We were very, very scared of the T-rex.

We found some eggs on the floor. It looked like they had fallen out of the tree. We picked one up and ran.

The mum and dad flew in the sky and the dad blew fire out of his mouth. It landed in the tree. We were not hurt.

Then we heard someone calling, 'Olivia, Sonny, it's teatime.'

We found the time machine and went home. We lived happily ever after.

OLIVIA SHAW (6)
KETTERING SCIENCE ACADEMY, KETTERING

GABRIEL'S JUNGLE STORY

Once upon a jungle, it was dark and especially quiet. Thirteen wolves spotted a scrumptious python so they snuck up to the tree.

The little python woke up in fear and slithered to his daddy python but the daddy python heard a noise then he woke up and saw the wolves and started to fight them.

A few minutes later, a fierce orange lion came out of green spiky thorn bushes.

The lion didn't know which way to go then he remembered what it sounded like in his village, his village was in the middle of the jungle. It sounded like a lake.

He listened both ways but it was the right path that was his home village. He was standing on a log then as quick as a flash, he was in his house. It turned to day and the wolves had run away and it all was happy.

GABRIEL ASHCROFT (6)

NEWTON BURGOLAND PRIMARY SCHOOL, COALVILLE

JULIE'S MAGICAL STORY

Once upon a time, there was a castle. In the castle lived unicorns. The dragon wanted to be a unicorn.

The dragon was sad because he wanted the witch to turn him into a unicorn.

The dragon saw the unicorn. The witch turned him into a unicorn.

The witch said, 'Now you will live with the unicorns forever.'

The witch went home. Everyone lived happily ever after.

JULIE GRACE NUTTING (5)

NEWTON BURGOLAND PRIMARY SCHOOL, COALVILLE

WILL'S DINOSAUR STORY

I am a famous artist and I travel to Dinosaur Land back in time, in my time machine.

Once, when I was at Dinosaur Land, I was playing games with some of the dinosaurs and then suddenly a whole forest of trees fell over and the trees knocked over a plant eater!

A giant, fierce T-rex came. The T-rex roared at me and I ran away and hid.

I climbed up a tree and I saw a nest full of eggs. The tree was a very big tree, even bigger than the T-rex. I didn't know what kind of dinosaur was in the eggs.

Suddenly, a giant pteranodon flew down and the eggs began to hatch. It squawked at me. I climbed down the tree and ran away.

At last the adventure was over. When I got home I painted everything that I saw on my adventure.

WILL GOODHEW (5)
NEWTON BURGOLAND PRIMARY SCHOOL, COALVILLE

JACK'S DINOSAUR STORY

I am the famous scientist, Freddo Bars, I am going to travel back in time to the dinosaurs.

These dinosaurs are impressive and exciting. They smell and they are very fierce.

This T-rex is scary and its eggs are creepy. I got a bit scared so I ran away.

These eggs are cracking. I wonder what they will be? Oh no, it's a pterodactyl!

Oh no! Mummy is coming, I'd better be off!

Phew, I'm home again. I had lots of fun and I'll remember those dinosaurs, that T-rex sure was creepy!

JACK JAGO SAXTY WATSON (6)
NEWTON BURGOLAND PRIMARY SCHOOL, COALVILLE

GRACE'S MAGICAL STORY

In Rainbow Castle lived a beautiful fair-haired princess called Grace. Grace loved chocolate ice cream and Yorkshire pudding with sausages. Outside, to protect the princess lived a dragon called Nigel.

He was fantastic at protecting! But he was bored and wanted to play with his unicorn friend, Annie. Nigel was friendly when most dragons were ferocious. Nigel was handsome; he had big green eyes and fantastic bright red scales. His wings were covered in tiny spots that sparkled in the sun; his tail was magnificent, like a long snake's body. Nigel went to dragon school to learn how to fly and breathe fire. Nigel loved the castle and the beautiful princess, he didn't want to be a fire dragon. He dreamed of living in a house with Annie the unicorn and inviting Princess Grace for her favourite snack, he thought Yorkshire pudding was yuck!

Nigel met with Annie. Annie had a brilliant day. 'I will take you to see Elma the witch and Sweeps, her very clever broom.'

Sweeps knew Nigel was bored and said, 'Follow me.'

He knew that the dragon and unicorn were great friends, he came up with an idea. He said, 'You can both stay with us.'

Nigel said, 'Thank you but I can't leave my princess just because I've been daydreaming.'

Nigel went home because it was the right thing to do.

GRACE COLE (5)
NEWTON BURGOLAND PRIMARY SCHOOL, COALVILLE

LUCAS' DINOSAUR STORY

I went in the time machine and I set it to the past, about 1,000,000 years ago.

When I got to my destination I saw a volcano going to erupt but the dinosaurs didn't care because they were too busy eating grass.

Then a T-rex stomped up to me. It was terrifying. He looked angry. 'Help... '

I wanted to save some eggs from hot lava and being eaten by the hungry T-rex.

Just in time the mother swooped down and rescued her eggs.

Time for me to go too. Home at last.

LUCAS EDWARDS (5)

NEWTON BURGOLAND PRIMARY SCHOOL, COALVILLE

MAY'S MAGICAL STORY

Once upon a time so long ago, so far away, lived a princess and her name was Beauty.

One day, a fierce dragon came to the castle and his name was Clordeen.

The dragon lit the castle on fire, then the dragon went to the woods and met a unicorn.

He put a stick on his head and pretended to be a unicorn so he could meet her.

The witch saw what had happened and so she ran.

She told the wand to turn the dragon into a real unicorn but the wand did not. He jumped out of her hands and went to the town.

He went to every home and told everyone about the wicked witch and the fierce dragon and everyone lived happily ever after.

MAY ELIZA MINDERIDES (6)
NEWTON BURGOLAND PRIMARY SCHOOL, COALVILLE

PHOEBE'S MAGICAL STORY

Once there was a beautiful pink castle. There were three purple flags that waved in the wind. Above the castle was a pretty rainbow that sparkled in the sky. In the castle lived a fierce fire-breathing dragon. Everyone in the village was terrified of the dragon.

The dragon was the most fierce fire-breathing dragon in all the land. When he was angry he breathed fire on everything in his way.

One day he was walking through the forest and he met a gorgeous unicorn with shimmering eyes. The dragon wanted to get married to the unicorn, but she was too scared. The good witch sent her magical broomstick to make the fierce dragon into a friendly dragon.

The unicorn and the dragon got married. The magical broomstick took them to a magical house on a hill where the moon shone brightly and they lived happily ever after.

PHOEBE DAVIES (6)
NEWTON BURGOLAND PRIMARY SCHOOL, COALVILLE

OLIVIA'S UNDER THE SEA STORY

It started as just another ordinary day sailing in my boat, when, all of a sudden, there was a loud 'whoosh!' of whistling wind, which flung me into the salty sea with a soggy splash!

Amazed, I opened my eyes to find myself in a wonderful, watery, undersea world.

'Hello,' said a friendly crab. 'I'm Snapper and this is my friend, Fingers the fish. Pleased to meet you!'

Suddenly, Snapper and Fingers disappeared as a terrifying, toothy shark approached. 'Oh no! Here comes the shark again. Help! Help! My friends and I are so, so scared of him!'

'Boo hoo, boo hoo, please don't go away. I just want some friends but everyone is so frightened of me!' the shark cried.

'But we thought you were going to eat us!'

Suddenly, a mermaid swooped in from under the coral.

I said, 'Be friends guys. Let's have an amazing party.' So we did.

The octopus orchestra played, the crab carolled, whilst the dolphins danced, the lobster let loose and the fish feasted on fish cakes.

'Wow!' said my undersea friends. 'That was the best party ever. Thank you for your help. Please come and see us again!'

So I returned to the boat and went home to write my terrific tale for you to read!

OLIVIA FRANCES SPENCER (7)
NEWTON BURGOLAND PRIMARY SCHOOL, COALVILLE

REBECCA'S MAGICAL STORY

A beautiful castle stood proudly on top of a light green hill. In the castle was a beautiful princess. This young princess spent her days dreaming about having a unicorn as a pet.

Sadly, the princess was trapped in the castle. The poor princess was held prisoner by a fierce dragon. Angrily, the dragon stomped around outside of the castle. A nasty witch had put a spell on the creature to make him do this.

One day, the beautiful princess decided to try to escape. Sneakily, the stunning princess dressed up as a magical unicorn and tried to get past the dragon who was breathing burning fire.

Suddenly, the dragon saw the beautiful unicorn. Instead of breathing angry fire, he felt very peaceful and happy.

Finally, the spell was broken and the dragon began to change. Slowly, he became a unicorn as he had seen what he really was when he saw the princess in the unicorn costume.

The witch was not in control anymore. The princess took off her costume and stroked the unicorn as a pet. She was free and the witch had vanished from her life.

REBECCA HARVEY (6)
NEWTON BURGOLAND PRIMARY SCHOOL, COALVILLE

SETH'S DINOSAUR STORY

They went back in time to the land of dinosaurs. It had trees and volcanoes. The volcanoes were hot and stinky. Dinosaurs lived a long, long time ago. We can only find dinosaurs' fossils now. Dinosaurs' fossils are buried in the ground a long, long way away. The remains are buried in the ground.

There was a big dinosaur called a T-rex. He was chomping some delicious leaves. He had sharp teeth and big eyes. T-rexes are big and scary.

The eggs needed to be warm and safe. The eggs needed to be with their mummy. The nest was very warm.

Pterodactyls are the only dinosaurs that can fly in the past. Pterodactyls are the best dinosaurs that fly.

They went back home on the time machine. They lived happily ever after.

SETH HOWLING (6)
NEWTON BURGOLAND PRIMARY SCHOOL, COALVILLE

GEORGIE'S SPACE STORY

Once upon a time, there was a spaceship coming back from the moon. Then the astronaut heard something weird.

Just then something fell off the spaceship. It was a rocket booster. The astronaut was very nervous. The rocket was near home but it couldn't get there.

Then the astronaut saw another ship. He thought there were bad aliens in the ship.

Just then a good alien came out of the ship. 'Hello,' it said.

The alien saw the broken rocket booster. He said, 'Shall I bring it home for you?'

'Yes please,' said the astronaut.

The alien brought the astronaut's rocket home for him.

'Thank you,' said the astronaut.

GEORGIE GOODHEW (7)
NEWTON BURGOLAND PRIMARY SCHOOL, COALVILLE

PETER'S DINOSAUR STORY

I built a time machine and went to the time of the dinosaurs.
When I got there, I saw a volcano exploding and the dinosaurs were running away.
Suddenly, a T-rex appeared roaring at me so I had to run away because the T-rex chased me.
I found a tree and I climbed up so the T-rex couldn't get me. I found a nest with three eggs. They were white and I wondered what dinosaur could be inside them.
In the sky I saw a pterodactyl flying around, looking for the three eggs. It knocked me back to the ground.
I ran back to the time machine and it took me home to my garden. I went inside and had a drink with my family.

PETER SIMON-STRONG BURTON (6)
NEWTON BURGOLAND PRIMARY SCHOOL, COALVILLE

Oscar's Jungle Story

It was dark in the jungle.
The snake was in the tree sleeping.
Then a scary snake said, 'Hssss!'
The lion was very scared.
The lion ran away.
The lion went home.

Oscar Jason Minderides (6)

Newton Burgoland Primary School, Coalville

GEORGE'S DINOSAUR STORY

I found a time machine to go back in time with and my time machine took me to see real dinosaurs such as a T-rex. Dinosaurs lived 300 years ago.

When I got to the land of dinosaurs, I saw a diplodocus and a stegosaurus. A volcano erupted and I ran away into the gigantic bushes and grass.

I saw a T-rex in the leaves and I was scared. I was very worried and ran away to a bird's nest.

In the bird's nest I saw three eggs. Suddenly one of the eggs hatched and the baby pterodactyl gave me a big hug and called me mummy, when I wasn't his mummy.

Suddenly, I saw something flying in the sky, it was the pterosaur's mummy and daddy. I went back to my time machine and it took me home.

When I got home, I thought to myself, *that was a very scary adventure.* I ran inside and went to bed.

GEORGE JAMES-STRONG BURTON (6)
NEWTON BURGOLAND PRIMARY SCHOOL, COALVILLE

Jonty's Dinosaur Story

I'm Professor Dontasaurus and I'm going back in time on my amazing time machine that I made to see the dinosaurs.

After a tremendously exciting journey, at last I got there. I saw lots of different kinds of dinosaurs. I saw an enormous volcano. It was just about to erupt.

Next, I saw a fierce, frightening T-rex. I was terrified. It stamped towards me. I hid behind some bushes. I could see the terrifying T-rex's foot next to me, it was monstrous! It could smell eggs in some trees. The T-rex could just reach. I could see a pterodactyl flying fast towards its nest and it was screeching at the T-rex.

It wrapped its wings around its nest to protect the eggs and used its beak to peck at the top of the T-rex's nose.

The T-rex was furious and stomped and roared. I escaped back to my time machine and flew back to the future. I'm never going back there again!

Jonty Norman (6)
Newton Burgoland Primary School, Coalville

AMBER'S UNDER THE SEA STORY

Once upon a time, there lived a family. There was a dad, mum, a girl and a boy. They went on holiday to France. First they booked a hotel, then they went sailing.

Under the water lived some happy sea creatures. The creatures were called Amy, Sam, Justin and Ranjeet.

One day under the sea, lived a vicious shark who was looking for the mermaid. Two hours later, the shark found her.

Luckily, King Triton came just in time and King Triton said, 'Get away from my daughter!' and the shark swam away as fast as he could. No one saw him again and they had a party to celebrate.

At the party, lots of creatures arrived and they had some delicious food, some awesome drinks and Amy, Justin, Ranjeet and Sam were there as well.

Then everyone went up to the surface and they waved at the people on the beach and the mom and dad and the children waved as well. They lived happily ever after.

AMBER DILKES (7)
NEWTON BURGOLAND PRIMARY SCHOOL, COALVILLE

BILLY'S DINOSAUR STORY

Once upon a time, there lived an inventor who invented a time machine and accidentally put the arrow to the past and it took him to the time of the dinosaurs.

When he got there he saw dinosaurs. 'Oh no, I have brought myself back to the time when the dinosaurs lived.'

Soon he saw a T-rex. He ran and he ran and bumped into a tree. He climbed up the tree and the T-rex ran past. 'Phew!' he said.

Then he saw a nest of eggs, one was starting to crack. One was bigger than him. It was gigantic.

The egg was opening and it was a pterodactyl. He grabbed the inventor and flew him to the time machine.

The inventor put the arrow on 'present' and it took him back home. He kissed the ground and went in his house for dinner.

BILLY HART (6)
NEWTON BURGOLAND PRIMARY SCHOOL, COALVILLE

LILY-ROSE'S DINOSAUR STORY

One day, a time machine landed in my garden. I was surprised! It wasn't there yesterday, maybe it fell from the sky?

It took me to the land of dinosaurs in the past. I was scared and frightened. I ran away because the volcano was erupting! The dinosaurs didn't care because they were too busy eating grass. Suddenly, a tyrannosaurus appeared through a bush, I was scared, I ran away.

I saw some eggs, not just eggs, pterodactyl eggs! As I watched, the eggs began to hatch. The baby pterodactyls popped out.

Next, mummy pterodactyl swooped down from the sky. I was very afraid. She smiled and said, 'Hello.'

I said, 'Hello my name is Lily-Rose.' I got into the time machine. It took me home. I landed in my garden. Wow, what an adventure! What will happen tomorrow?

LILY-ROSE ROBINSON-SMITH (6)

NEWTON BURGOLAND PRIMARY SCHOOL, COALVILLE

Jimmy's Dinosaur Story

I was playing outside on a hot summer's day, when me and my brother, Lewis, went in the dark shed and found a time machine covered in cobwebs.

We decided to sit on it, when suddenly it took us to the land of the dinosaurs. We were scared but excited too. We saw a spotty dinosaur with a long neck, he looked like a gentle giant. 'Look,' said Lewis, 'a dinosaur with plates and spikes all over his back!'

'Oh no!' I shouted. 'An enormous T-rex is coming! Quick Lewis, hide!' We climbed up a massive tree. 'Phew!' I said. 'That was close!'

After the T-rex had gone, we looked around at the huge branches and discovered a nest with green dinosaur eggs inside.

All of a sudden, the eggs were beginning to hatch. 'Wow!' said Lewis. A baby pterodactyl crawled out the egg.

'Hello,' I said. This was a friendly dinosaur. We stroked him before he flew away. 'We had better go home, Mum will be worried,' I said.

We climbed back down the tree and sat on the time machine. Finally, we were back in our garden.

'What an adventure!' we laughed.

Jimmy Aldridge (7)
Newton Burgoland Primary School, Coalville

FREYA'S MAGICAL STORY

Once upon a time, lived a princess who had hair as long as string. Her eyes were as shiny as gold, her dress was as sparkly as jewels. She had a pretty castle but a dragon wanted the castle to himself so he had a plan to burn the castle to get rid of the princess and have the castle to himself.

So the dragon started flaming. The princess called her unicorn but the dragon still didn't stop. The princess called her unicorn again, soon it came.

The unicorn stared as she fought. It was hard for her though she carried on. She was almost out of breath when a witch came.

She got out her wand and began to join in. She was laughing evilly, the princess was horrified by her.

Soon she sent her wand to recharge so it did but it never came back. Where did it go?

FREYA GANT

OLD DALBY CE PRIMARY SCHOOL, MELTON MOWBRAY

MELISSA'S MAGICAL STORY

Once upon a time, there lived two unicorns, their names were Anna and Sunshine, they had magic powers. Their powers were sunshine and ice.

One day, a witch sent her dragon. It was trying to get the unicorns. The friends tried to defeat him, but he kept breathing fire. They used their powers but it didn't work, but they did not give up.

Suddenly, the dragon went up to the unicorns and they used their feet to defend each other.

Also the witch had a magic paintbrush for her wand and she cast a spell on Sunshine.

Then the witch magicked them both home and they all lived happily ever after.

MELISSA LOUISE HATLEY (7)
OLD DALBY CE PRIMARY SCHOOL, MELTON MOWBRAY

OLIVIA'S SPACE STORY

My rocket is flying over the moon and some stars twinkle past me.
Something has fallen off. My rocket has flown past the world and we
have to land on the moon.
A spaceship flies around the stars and moon and goes past.
An alien inside says, 'Could I help you?'
So he brings his rocket and he takes me home.

OLIVIA STAFFORD (4)
OLD DALBY CE PRIMARY SCHOOL, MELTON MOWBRAY

JORJI'S JUNGLE STORY

Once in a jungle there was a snake called Sailab. He was very kind and helpful. On Thursday he saw some trees. As he walked into the trees, he saw lots of little eyes and he saw one tiny thing fly out of the trees. 'It's bats,' he said.

Sailab saw another snake. He had very sharp teeth. His name was Liso. He had a very long, red tongue.

Then in one minute Liso saw a lion called Leo. Leo was very strong. 'Leo to the rescue!' he said.

He ran and ran and while he was running he picked up a thorn and stabbed the thorn in Liso's neck and then he saved Sailab.

Then Leo ran back to the jungle and went to sleep in his own little, tiny, small bed then they had a very big party.

JORJI KLEIN LEAVIS (6)
OLD DALBY CE PRIMARY SCHOOL, MELTON MOWBRAY

NOAH'S SPACE STORY

Once upon a time, there was a rocket and the rocket was taking off.
It was above the Earth.
You could see the stars and the moon. The rocket had fire coming out.
There was a face peering out of the holes in the moon and it was an
alien, it was a blue alien. It had one hundred eyes.
The spaceman put a space flag in the moon.
The rocket was landing and it had tiny windows.
The spaceman was wearing a helmet.

NOAH KLEIN LEAVIS (6)
OLD DALBY CE PRIMARY SCHOOL, MELTON MOWBRAY

MATHEUS' SPACE STORY

In my adventure I was going to Planet Mars. The planet looked cool to me.

I was flying around Earth, it looked amazing in space. The stars were twinkling.

When I was flying I saw a UFO in space. It was coming straight at me. An alien came out of the UFO. The alien had three eyes and he had four fingers.

The UFO took me and the rocket back to Earth and it was a long trip back to Earth.

Soon we arrived back home. When we got back it was night-time.

MATHEUS RUFUS (6)
PARKLANDS PRIMARY SCHOOL, NORTHAMPTON

SONNY'S SPACE STORY

Daddy and I made a rocket in the garage.
We took off in the rocket into space to look for Mars.
We saw a spaceship fly by and an alien waved at us.
His name was Mip and he was nice.
He beamed us up and took us to Mars for tea.
Then Mip beamed us home for milk and biscuits before bed.

SONNY LAWRENCE (6)
PARKLANDS PRIMARY SCHOOL, NORTHAMPTON

JOE'S SPACE STORY

Deep in space there was a rocket, a dark red rocket. This super powerful rocket was on a long journey from Earth to Mars.

All of a sudden, the power ceased and the rocket crash-landed on Jupiter. The astronauts inside the dark red rocket felt horrified and looked petrified.

At first they thought there was a bright shooting star heading towards them, but as it got closer they realised it was a UFO. The astronauts wished they could start up the engine but they could not.

Through the window they saw a green three-eyed alien. It had a funny smiley face.

The rocket shook and so did the astronauts, so much they felt sick. 'Someone help me! The rocket's shaking,' squealed one of the astronauts.

The other one screamed, 'I am too young to die! Someone help us!'

A voice came out of the radio nice and clear. 'No need to be scared. I'm just helping you get back to Earth,' said the three-eyed alien. The alien beamed the dark red rocket back to Earth.

JOE CUMING (7)
PARKLANDS PRIMARY SCHOOL, NORTHAMPTON

Izzy's Space Story

One day, I went to space to meet my space friends and see the aliens, also to see all different planets: Mars, Earth, Jupiter, Pluto, Saturn, Uranus, etc.

We explored the whole of space then discovered the black hole. One of my friends got sucked up in the black hole and we all tried to pull her out, but it was no use.

Then we saw a spaceship and got distracted and in there was a superhero and she saved my friend.

When we got in the ship we had hot chocolate and biscuits. Then she took us to her hideout. We slept at her house.

The next day we met her friends and stayed at her friend Milly's house. For lunch we had fresh salad, we had lettuce in it, carrots, cabbage, tomato, cucumber and lots of other things, yum-yum.

After lunch we played together then it was time to go home to bed. What a long day!

Izzy Earl (7)
Parklands Primary School, Northampton

LOLA'S SPACE STORY

One day, I asked my mum if I could go to the moon and she said, 'Yes you can.'

I got into my rocket and counted down to zero and blasted off! I went to the moon.

I saw a spaceship landing on the moon, it was blue, orange and pink. It was surrounded by pretty stars.

Then I saw a lion, he was green and he was smiling and he waved at me.

The spaceship flew above the rocket flashing its bright lights.

The spaceship guided the rocket safely. I loved my trip to the moon.

LOLA SKIPWORTH (6)
PARKLANDS PRIMARY SCHOOL, NORTHAMPTON

DAISY'S SPACE STORY

When I lay in bed at night I wonder what space might look like! I close my eyes and imagine I am floating among the stars and see the moon...
The moon has a smiling face. He says, 'Hello, how are you?' and I ask him how he is too.
Out the corner of my eye I see a UFO. It is bright and shiny.
Suddenly the doors open and a little alien pops out. He shouts, 'Hi, do you want to come for a ride with me?'
I say, 'Yes please.' I am suddenly beamed up! I can see shining light, reds, blues and greens.
I realise that the UFO is taking me home. I float for a while then I wake up and think, *wow!*

DAISY BURRELL (6)
PARKLANDS PRIMARY SCHOOL, NORTHAMPTON

MY TRIP TO THE MOON

One day I decided to build a rocket and I went to the moon.
It took me 20 minutes to get the moon.
When I got to the moon I saw a spaceship. It was big and bright.
As I got out of the rocket I saw an alien. He had three eyes and a big mouth. He looked funny.
The alien took my rocket with his special laser.
He beamed me back home. I miss the moon and the alien.

REECE CORLESS (7)
PARKLANDS PRIMARY SCHOOL, NORTHAMPTON

ADAM'S SPACE STORY

There was once a boy that went to space, his name was Billy Race.
He had made his own rocket because he wanted to know what space looked like.

He was travelling through space drawing pictures of the planets.
Suddenly, an alien spaceship hit Billy's rocket and it crashed onto Mars.
Billy looked out of his rocket's window and saw an alien spaceship next to his rocket, Billy was scared.

A friendly alien came out of the spaceship, he had three eyes. He said, 'Sorry I hit your rocket, can I help you?'

Billy said, 'Yes please, take me home,'

The alien said, 'Don't worry, I will take you home.' A large beam of light appeared onto Billy's rocket.

The alien spaceship carried Billy's rocket safely to his home, Planet Earth. Billy waved goodbye to the alien's spaceship.

ADAM KHERRY (7)

PARKLANDS PRIMARY SCHOOL, NORTHAMPTON

KNOJAH'S SPACE STORY

One day, I saw a rocket. Then I went inside the rocket and it blasted off into space. It went to the moon and I saw some stars, I went all the way to the moon and it was scary when I got there. What frightened me was the dark.

Then a bit fell off the rocket and landed on the ground. I got out of the rocket and looked at the bit that had fallen off and I knew that I was in trouble.

All of a sudden, a spaceship appeared. The spaceship landed on the ground and I found an alien and that alien was friendly.

'Hello,' said the alien.

'What's your name?' I asked and he said it was Jack. Then I thought about his three eyes and his three teeth with his mouth open.

'My spaceship doesn't work,' said Jack.

I said, 'You could come with us. Then I will take you back to your home.'

Me and Jack got onto the spaceship and we blasted off. Then we got to Jack's home and the alien said thank you. He got out of the spaceship. Jack went inside his house and called me to come in.

KNOJAH KOGULAVARATHAN (7)

PARKLANDS PRIMARY SCHOOL, NORTHAMPTON

JASMINE'S SPACE STORY

I went to space, I caught a rocket from a town, I went with Amy, Steven and Mummy.

Inside the rocket we all had cucumber sandwiches and chocolate cake, tap water and orange juice.

We set off to outer space, to a place called Neptune. When we landed on Neptune we met an alien called Bob.

He looked like an octopus, he was green and slimy and spoke Neptunean. He enjoyed our cucumber sandwiches.

He invited us to have a ride in his spaceship. It went fast and it was fun.

Soon it was time to go home. We said goodbye to Bob.

JASMINE LOASBY-COOK (7)
PARKLANDS PRIMARY SCHOOL, NORTHAMPTON

VINCENT'S SPACE STORY

Hi, I am Vincent. I travel across the universe finding new planets and galaxies.

One night I set off. It was gloomy, dull and dark. Finally I got to Mars, the planet I was hoping to get to. It was over 600,000 miles, that's even longer than my house to Nan's house!

Suddenly, a UFO (AKA an unidentifiable flying object) came flying straight for me. 'Argh!' I screamed and ran.

The alien jumped out of the spaceship and... started smiling and waving and said, 'Hello human life form.'

Really he was here to help me get back to Earth because my ship had broken and the engine had fallen off.

After a good game of space invaders, he helped me to get to Earth. I said, 'Thank you I will come and see you again.' We both lived happily ever after.

VINCENT ROSE (7)
PARKLANDS PRIMARY SCHOOL, NORTHAMPTON

ISABELLA'S STORY

Once upon a time, there was a girl called Abby. She loved her toy Elsa but all she wanted was to go in a forest. Her mum always said no. She wished her dream would come true.

But that night, Abby woke up and she was in a forest with Elsa and Elsa was alive. Abby couldn't believe her eyes.

Abby saw a big house and went inside it but there was nobody there. Abby and Elsa were all alone but then they saw someone coming and he said, 'Who are you?'

Abby and Elsa didn't say a word because Abby's mum said don't speak to strangers, but then Abby said, 'Can we stay with you?'

The person said, 'Yes. My name is Bailly and I have a brother called Jenson. Are you sisters?'

Abby and Elsa said, 'No, we are BFFs.'

Bailly said, 'Do you want me to take you home?'

Abby said, 'Yes.'

So Bailly said, 'Home, home,' and Abby was back home.

ISABELLA DOHERTY (7)
PARKLANDS PRIMARY SCHOOL, NORTHAMPTON

TAYLOR'S SPACE STORY

The broken rocket was flying out of control around the Planet Bobohoeba.

The alien inside was going to have to make a crash-landing.

Zob, the alien, climbed out of the rocket to look at the damage. He was going to need help from a pick-up ship.

A friendly, three-eyed monster mechanic called ZingZang, came to help. ZingZang transported the rocket back to Zob's home using his rocket laser light.

ZingZang was invited back to Zob's house for a dinner of burgers as a thank you for helping him.

TAYLOR SKATES (6)
PARKLANDS PRIMARY SCHOOL, NORTHAMPTON

ABBY'S SPACE STORY

Once I had a dream that I zoomed off to Mars. I travelled in a spaceship in my PJs and it had a hot chocolate machine inside.

When I was in space I looked out the port hole and I saw a great big blue marble, it was the Earth.

As I travelled through space I saw a funny-looking spaceship. It was green all over.

I peered through the window, I saw a green alien, he had three eyes and he was friendly.

Then suddenly a bright beam appeared over me. It came from the alien spaceship. He said, 'Come on, I'll take you home.'

I was tired by the time I got home so I got into bed. Then I woke up from my dream and had some breakfast.

ABBY WADE (7)
PARKLANDS PRIMARY SCHOOL, NORTHAMPTON

OSCAR'S SPACE STORY

I made a spaceship out of Minecraft blocks. I jumped in my rocket and went to Minecraft World.

I flew around the galaxy and saw Minecraft World.

I saw a spaceship and it looked huge and it was shooting a laser at my spaceship.

The person who was in the ship was an Enderman, it had purple ears and green eyes and it was big.

But it was good and I went inside his ship and had lunch and he carried me and my ship home.

I had my tea.

OSCAR MORRISON (6)
PARKLANDS PRIMARY SCHOOL, NORTHAMPTON

TAMIKA'S SPACE STORY

Once upon a time, there lived a girl called Alice. She found a rocket, it was big and red.

Then she met a boy called David.

Alice said, 'Do you want to go in my rocket?'

David said, 'Yes.'

So they went in and they pressed a button and they went up and up but then they stopped.

They put their space clothes on and went out. Alice did a cartwheel, David did a roly-poly.

The spaceship fell down so Alice had an idea. 'We could push it up.' And it worked.

TAMIKA MATIKA (6)

PARKLANDS PRIMARY SCHOOL, NORTHAMPTON

ALEENA'S SPACE STORY

When it was the school holidays, me and my brother decided to make
a rocket. Our dad helped to make the rocket, our mum cooked some
food to take it with us.

When the rocket was ready, we went inside and made sure everything
was working fine.

We went to space. We stopped on a planet. We went outside. We saw
an alien. He was a very friendly alien.

He said he could give us a tour of the planet, so we went with him. It
was a very pretty place. We took some pictures to show it to Mum
and Dad. Everybody looked very happy on that planet.

We played with the alien. We had a great time. It was getting late and
we were feeling hungry, so we decided to go back to the rocket.

We shared our food with the alien, he liked our food. We said goodbye
to the alien. He was very sad, we missed him too. We reached home
safely. What an adventure we had.

ALEENA JIJI (6)
PARKLANDS PRIMARY SCHOOL, NORTHAMPTON

MOLLY'S SPACE STORY

I blasted into space in my big rocket ship and I saw lots of stars shining around the moon.

I went round the Earth and landed on the moon safely.

Suddenly, I saw a UFO and it landed right beside me.

The door opened and out came a friendly alien. His name was Wiggly and he said, 'Nice to meet you.'

I asked Wiggly if he could take me and my rocket home because it crash-landed and couldn't fly.

So Wiggly dropped me off home safely and we waved goodbye.

MOLLY REED (7)

PARKLANDS PRIMARY SCHOOL, NORTHAMPTON

MEGAN'S SPACE STORY

The moon sparkles and gas comes out of the rocket. *Zoom, zoom!*
The Earth looks beautiful when the rocket goes past the stars.
Soon, another rocket comes so we have a look inside.
It is an alien, it runs at us and laughs.
The big rocket is under the spaceship. What is it doing there?
The spaceship is shining a light on the rocket to find its way home.

MEGAN UNDERWOOD (6)

PARKLANDS PRIMARY SCHOOL, NORTHAMPTON

SALVATORE'S SPACE STORY

One day, I saw a rocket and the door was opened. Then I went inside for an adventure. I flew to space heading towards the moon.

I flew all around the moon. Then I landed with a terrible crash. A side of my rocket had been destroyed. My heart was pounding with fear because I was on my own.

A few minutes later, I saw a spaceship which was passing by. I turned on my rocket for attention with a flashing light. The spaceship luckily saw me.

A funny, smiley alien with three-eyes, came out and he asked me what had happened. I told him that I'd crashed and I couldn't fly my rocket anymore.

After that, he advised me to stay inside my rocket. Then he lifted me up with a magnetic power and I wondered how he did it.

The spaceship was very fast and in a few minutes we were back on Earth. I was amazed how he landed me beside my house. It was an awesome adventure.

SALVATORE RENDINA (7)
PARKLANDS PRIMARY SCHOOL, NORTHAMPTON

REGINALD'S SPACE STORY

Saturday morning, I was in my back garden playing football. I said to my little brother, 'I don't want to play football, I want to go to outer space.'

'But we're not real spacemen, or are we?'

'No, we're not.'

'Okay, let's ask Dad if we can play in the shed.'

'Okay.'

'Dad, can we play in the shed?'

'Okay, but be careful.'

'Okay Dad.'

We got some milk and juice cartons and used them for buttons for our spaceship and got some sticks for levers. 'There,' my little brother said, 'our rocket ship is complete. We can turn on the pretend rocket ship.' But it wasn't pretend. It blasted to Mars. We got hungry so we ate Mars bars (get it? We're on Mars and we're eating Mars bars?). We walked and walked and walked until we saw an alien. We said hi. He said hi back.

He was hungry so we gave him one of our Mars bars. He snuck away and he went back to his master and told him humans were on Mars. The monster said to invade Earth using a giant robot to attack. 'I hate humans with their fancy clothes and those things that move. We shall attack Earth tomorrow morning. I will tell everyone on Mars. We shall begin the planning phase.'

I overheard them saying they were going to take over the Earth. I said to my little brother, 'We've got to do something.' We snuck in and quickly ran through the guards. We snuck up behind the king and put him in a sack and we ran and my little brother took the guards out. We took their suits and walked carefully along the wall. Another guard asked, 'What's in the sack?'

I said, 'An intruder.'

'Okay, kick him out the castle.'

'Okay.'

So we left the castle and kicked him into cyber space and he accidentally went into the Milky Way and got transported to dimension X.

One guard saw us so we ran into the spaceship and switched on the spaceship and blasted back to Earth to have dinner so my mum didn't get worried about us. We are never ever going to tell anyone and I mean anyone. What an adventure we had!

REGINALD NATHAN MAJWEGA (7)

PARKLANDS PRIMARY SCHOOL, NORTHAMPTON

JOSHUA'S SPACE STORY

I went to space in a tall spaceship. I went to the mission control room. Just then I landed on the moon! I found a space shuttle, it had a satellite.

I drove it to two craters. I found rocks that looked like bricks and I built a moon base.

I built a shed for my space buggy. Just then I heard a knock at the door.

Bang! Bang! 'What was that?' I opened the door and at the door was an alien.

I became friends with him. We played hide-and-seek. Bedtime!

JOSHUA WATTS (6)
PARKLANDS PRIMARY SCHOOL, NORTHAMPTON

EVAN'S SPACE STORY

Once there was a little boy that loved space so much that it was all he ever talked about.

One day, he went to a space station on a school trip and found a door that said: 'Staff only'. He opened the door, not noticing the sign.

Inside there was a big rocket getting prepared to launch. He hid inside it.

Soon he felt it moving. *Wow!* he thought, but looked out the window and it was just the motorway! What a shame, he thought he was going into space.

When he felt the rocket stop moving, he climbed out and saw that he was at a space exhibition which was just as good!

EVAN WILKINS (6)
PARKLANDS PRIMARY SCHOOL, NORTHAMPTON

ELLA'S SPACE STORY

I went to space on an adventure. It was big and wide. You had to wear a blue mask.

I landed on the sand, it was bumpy and wobbly and twisty and swirly. There were golden stars.

I wore a golden suit and suddenly bumped into an alien. I nearly got caught.

There was a house, I went in. There were lots of aliens, a million. They didn't give their mum a birthday card.

Their mum was sad so we made some cards and had a bit of cake.

It started to get dark so I put my spacesuit back on and flew home.

ELLA MAY LEE (6)
PARKLANDS PRIMARY SCHOOL, NORTHAMPTON

IGOR'S SPACE STORY

I would like to fly a rocket to the moon because I would like to admire the beautiful views of the Earth with a rocket. Perhaps among the stars meet a spaceship. I dream of such a meeting!

I saw an alien spaceship. I wondered what he looked like.

He had three eyes and he looked like a potato. He had sharp teeth. He was happy and funny!

He helped me take my rocket back to Earth. I had no fuel.

He took my rocket and flew with my rocket and took it back to my garden. It was a great time!

IGOR ZYLKA (6)

PARKLANDS PRIMARY SCHOOL, NORTHAMPTON

JOHN-PAUL'S SPACE STORY

Once upon a time, there was a spaceship. He flew from the moon and the stars.

His power was off then he went to pass Earth, then the spaceship went to pass the stars.

Then after that, an alien flew on his ship to Earth.

The alien had three eyes, a terrible tongue and he had three teeth.

The alien spaceship and the other rocket flew away all day long.

The spaceship and the alien flew the good rocket away again.

JOHN-PAUL MEAD (6)

PARKLANDS PRIMARY SCHOOL, NORTHAMPTON

THE KITTEN AND THE MAGIC LEMON TEA

Once upon a time, there was a princess kitten. She was white as snow and hyper and her name was White.

One day, White had a glass of lemon tea and it was magical because she turned into a mermaid with secret water powers.

If anyone was unkind or naughty, she had the power to make it rain on them, soggy and wet.

So everyone had to be really good because of the way the princess kitten ruled her kingdom using her secret lemon tea, it was the best place to live ever.

FEDERICA MENINNO-SYMONS (6)
PARKLANDS PRIMARY SCHOOL, NORTHAMPTON

ISABEL'S SPACE STORY

I want to go to space to adventure in the galaxy. I want to go to the sun to have a closer look at the sun. I want to go to Fire Land to put it out.

When I do all of these things I will be a busy bunny.

I want to go to Australia to visit the koalas. I want them to climb on me and treat me like a tree.

When I grow up I will look after animals like monkeys, birds and horses and donkeys, also animals that are hurt. I will give them food. I will give them water and animal drinks. I will touch spiders to keep them safe and elephants too.

I will be brave and touch big hairy spiders and I will look after the big wild monkeys.

ISABEL FLORENCE CLARK (6)
PARKLANDS PRIMARY SCHOOL, NORTHAMPTON

BERTIE'S SPACE STORY

I wanted to go to Mars in the rocket because it was red and it looked interesting.

I flew around Mars and I looked out the window. My wing fell off. I thought I was going to fall off the Earth.

Suddenly, I saw a flying saucer. It was coming very fast through the sky, I could just see it.

I heard a voice of a little green alien. He said, 'Do you need any help?' So I said, 'Yes, because my wing fell off in space.'

The alien said, 'I will get you home.' He gently lifted me off Mars back to Earth.

He did not know where my house was so I told him where it was. I said, 'Have some dinner at my house.'

BERTIE BOOTH
PARKLANDS PRIMARY SCHOOL, NORTHAMPTON

HARRY'S SPACE STORY

Deep, deep in space there was a chimp. His name was Chocolate the chimp.

He went round and round the Earth. He saw the Squiggly Land.

He saw some meteors. The chimp saw a thing flashing and it went very fast.

Then he landed on the moon. He saw an alien castle. He knocked on the door.

The aliens took him and the rocket. They teleported him into their UFO.

They took the chimp back home, his mummy was proud of him.

HARRY COOMBS

PARKLANDS PRIMARY SCHOOL, NORTHAMPTON

SAM'S SPACE STORY

One day, a man tried to go to the moon but something shot him down. 'What was that?' said the pilot. The pilot didn't know what hit him. The pilot got out of the ship and took a look at the damage. 'Oh no, the wing has broken off.' When the man got his tools, he saw something in a crater.

He went and shone his torch down the crater and inside the crater was a UFO. The UFO flew towards him and out came a slimy alien! Then man jumped back with excitement. The alien spoke to the man. 'I saw the damage to your ship. Do you want me to fix it?'

The alien picked up the ship with the UFO.

When they got to Earth, the man took a deep breath and went outside.

SAM BROADBENT (6)

PATTISHALL CE PRIMARY SCHOOL, TOWCESTER

BEN'S BRILLIANT ROCKET

Once upon a time, there was a man called Ben. Ben had a rocket. One day, Ben went to space. When he got to space one of the wings fell off!

So he landed on Scooby World. First he was scared but then he got used to it.

Then he saw something, it was spinning, it looked strange. It was strange, it was a flying saucer!

Next it landed. The door opened and a beam of light came out then a green figure came out, it was an alien!

Then it picked up my rocket, I couldn't see very much. It was weird that a huge rocket was getting sucked up by a small thing.

Next, that thing dropped me back at home and I lived happily ever after.

JACK GARDNER (7)
PATTISHALL CE PRIMARY SCHOOL, TOWCESTER

NADIA'S SPACE STORY

Once upon a time, there lived an alien. She went to the moon. The rocket crashed on a different planet.

She met another alien. When she saw the alien come out of the saucer she wanted to say hello.

She saw it fly all around the stars. It landed and she saw the alien, it had three eyes and a round body.

The first alien said hello. The other alien said hello. The alien with three eyes took the other alien in his saucer.

They flew to the three-eyed alien's house and they lived happily ever after.

NADIA RIBEIRO (6)
PATTISHALL CE PRIMARY SCHOOL, TOWCESTER

Sienna's Space Story

Once upon a time, there lived a huge rocket flying in space.
It was bright red and had yellow stripes and a huge window on the front.
Next, the rocket landed on the moon and there were massive circle holes so people could see through them.
Then something appeared from the sky and landed on the moon quickly.
It was a slobby alien as green as mint ice cream and the alien had three eyes and three really sharp teeth.
There were three bright stars as bright as the sun and there was a blue light shining down to the rocket.
And then they all headed home where they would be safe.

Sienna Ashleigh Richardson (7)
Pattishall CE Primary School, Towcester

ALFIE'S SPACE STORY

We went to space in a rocket.
When we got there we saw an alien, it was called Gloopy.
He was a bit silly. He was amazing.
We went home. It was great fun. 'Bye alien!' we said.

ALFIE NEWNHAM (7)

PATTISHALL CE PRIMARY SCHOOL, TOWCESTER

HARRY'S SPACE STORY

First there was a planet, on that planet was an alien. It was floppy and his arms were flexible. His eyes were massive, his teeth had seaweed between them. His floppy tongue was as long as a snake. His scaly skin could burn as bright as the sun. His tail was as long as a lorry. His nails were as giant as an eye. His body was bigger than a house. It was giant. It was the same size as a dinosaur. He could jump far and high. The giant alien had a nap then the next morning the giant alien set off for a stroll in the park. Finally, he had a bounce around the park.

Then a flying saucer came, it was round and red like a ball, it was giant. The giant alien bounced on the flying saucer then the flying saucer shook the giant alien, his sharp nails dug into the saucer. Out came an alien! It had three sharp teeth and it was cute. It said, 'Hello. I like you, you're different to me. You are giant and I am small. You have giant hands and I have small hands. You have two eyes and I have three eyes. I have a giant mouth, you have a small mouth. I need some help, my flying saucer is broken so can I have some help please?'

'Why not?' So the friends set off to fix the flying saucer.

They fixed the flying saucer then the rocket was broken, one of the bits had come off. Then the saucer lifted up. The saucer helped the rocket lift off the ground. The saucer did the most amazing thing.

Then after the amazing thing, it led the rocket to a house, not an ordinary house, to the alien's house where his children were sleeping.

HARRY ALSWORTH (7)
PATTISHALL CE PRIMARY SCHOOL, TOWCESTER

RUBY'S SPACE STORY

Once upon a time, there were people on a mission and one bit of the rocket had broken off but they still could fly.

Suddenly, the rocket crashed on the moon.

Afterwards, someone else arrived and it was an alien.

Then it said, 'Hello.'

The astronaut said, 'Argh!'

The alien took them back to Earth.

The man was fine, but the rocket was not fine.

RUBY LOUISE COLLINS (6)

PATTISHALL CE PRIMARY SCHOOL, TOWCESTER

SEREN'S SPACE STORY

Once upon a time, a girl called Silly Suesan, was on a mission to Jupiter but was afraid of aliens! 'I hate aliens!' shouted Suesan.

There were aliens on Jupiter but Suesan didn't know.

Suddenly, a huge spaceship appeared. It was red and topaz and yellow with a twist of green.

A purple alien appeared. It had three eyes and it was smiling and saying hello and Suesan started screaming.

The alien was nice and the rocket was broken so the alien helped. He was as helpful as a person helping a kitten.

So the alien put his carrying light on and carried the ship and Suesan home.

SEREN POWELL (6)

PATTISHALL CE PRIMARY SCHOOL, TOWCESTER

BETTY'S BEST PLACE TO GO AND HIDE

One dark, spooky night, Betty crept quietly into her rocket and blasted off to space. She was excited to see her alien friend again.

Betty flew higher than the clouds and into space. She looked and looked but Betty could not find her.

Then Betty saw something behind her, it was her friend Alien and when Alien got out she said, 'Boo!'

'Hello again friend,' said Betty. 'Let's go and play.'

'Alright, that will be fun,' said Alien.

'Let's go and play on Mars.'

'OK.'

'I am yawning,' said Betty.

'Then I'll give you a ride home.'

'Alright. First go down then left and straight on, left again and then right.'

'Now we're home, night-night friend, hope you enjoyed your day.'

'I did, bye-bye.'

PIPER MULLEN (7)

PATTISHALL CE PRIMARY SCHOOL, TOWCESTER

ALIENS ON EARTH

One day, there was a man called Ben. He woke up every day at 4 o'clock. He worked as a spaceman.

He got into his spaceship and counted down, 10, 9, 8, 7, 6, 5, 4, 3, 2, 1 blast-off!

It took him three days to get there and the moon was there. Ben landed on the moon.

He saw some people but they weren't people. It was an alien. 'Ha ha ha! Hi, I'm Flo.'

'Why don't you come back to Earth?' said Ben.

'OK. Do you mind if some friends come over?'

'Why not?'

100 aliens came out and they flew to Earth and lived happily ever after.

TYLER RILEY (7)
PATTISHALL CE PRIMARY SCHOOL, TOWCESTER

A TRIP TO SPACE

One night, some people blasted off to space past the stars and the sun. Soon after, they landed on the moon but their rocket was broken. One of the fins was snapped off.

But someone else was visiting the moon in a flying saucer.

Then an alien came out and waved hello but the people were scared so they ran to the rocket and locked the door.

Next, the alien climbed into his flying saucer and zapped the rocket into the air back to their house and into their garden without the people knowing.

GEORGE BRAND (7)

PATTISHALL CE PRIMARY SCHOOL, TOWCESTER

BEN AND THE GIANT ROCKET

Once there lived a boy called Ben. He really wanted to go to the moon. He had a bright red and yellow rocket. Once he thought, *I want to go to the moon.* He went off.

First he felt a bit queasy but he saw some stars and the bright moon! Then he set the rocket to stop on the moon. He smashed on the moon. Ben said, 'I can fly!'

Then Ben saw a spaceship and he thought there was an alien inside. The spaceship was green with bright yellow flashing lights.

The alien was bright green and it had three eyes. He had spiky teeth and a big red tongue. His name was Sam.

Sam sucked Ben up into the spaceship and Ben was scared. Sam talked to Ben and Ben didn't understand. He scared Ben and he tested Ben to see if he was from his planet.

He put Ben back in his garden and Ben got out of the spaceship. He went into his red house and said, 'That was fun.'

ROSIE BURT (7)
PATTISHALL CE PRIMARY SCHOOL, TOWCESTER

CHARLIE'S SPACE STORY

First some astronauts set off to the moon in their extraordinary rocket.

They finally landed on top of the rocky moon. They bounced out of the rocket and landed on the rough surface.

After that moment, they saw a shiny, silver flying saucer above their heads.

Next, they saw a gooey green alien. He was really scary and green.

Then the shiny flying saucer scanned the gleaming rocket.

Finally, the saucer placed the rocket back home.

CHARLIE MILLS (7)
PATTISHALL CE PRIMARY SCHOOL, TOWCESTER

THE BEAMING BOUNCY ROCKET

One Sunday, I went to get a new spaceship. Suddenly, I saw a beaming red, bouncy rocket!

I flew my new rocket to the cheesy moon, it had craters all around the moon. I landed with a big crash and broke it.

As quick as a flash, I jumped into a different spaceship but it wasn't mine, it was someone else's.

All of a sudden, an orange gloopy alien came. I thought, *I've seen her before. I think it is my mum,* but no, it couldn't be.

She lifted my spaceship, it was amazing. Her spaceship was so shiny.

It was my mum and she stayed with me forever and ever.

ISABELLA MAY NOTRIDGE (7)

PATTISHALL CE PRIMARY SCHOOL, TOWCESTER

THE CRASHED ROCKET

Once upon a time, there was a rocket. It went to the moon.
It got to it but suddenly their rocket crashed and they were waiting and waiting for someone to come.
A flying saucer came from nowhere.
And one hour later, an alien appeared from the saucer. 'Hi!' shouted the alien.
The flying saucer took the rocket back to Earth.

FREDDIE PATTERSON-SMITH (6)
PATTISHALL CE PRIMARY SCHOOL, TOWCESTER

KAIDI-LEE'S JUNGLE STORY

One day, Casey and Tom arrived at the jungle.

Then they saw a snake. They didn't know how to get out of the jungle.

The snake was nasty and scary. The snake was wild.

Suddenly, a lion appeared.

He ran after the snake.

Then he helped Casey and Tom get home.

KAIDI-LEI SHEEHAN (6)

QUEEN ELEANOR PRIMARY SCHOOL, NORTHAMPTON

MUNEEB'S JUNGLE STORY

Casey and Tom went to the jungle. They looked in there and they saw a snake.

The snake was a slimy snake. The snake was in the bushes.

They were scared because they thought he was going to eat them.

They saw a friendly lion. They hopped on to the lion. The lion was kind. The lion ran after the snake. The lion had a long tail. He was smiley. Then he got them home. 'Goodbye.'

MUNEEB UR REHMAN (6)

QUEEN ELEANOR PRIMARY SCHOOL, NORTHAMPTON

NIKITA'S JUNGLE STORY

One day, Tom and Casey went to the scary jungle. They wanted to go further until they saw a bad snake.

The snake was pretending to be a good snake.

Then they saw a friendly lion that said, 'Jump on my back to save your life.'

He ran and he ran but the snake was still chasing the lion.

After all that, the lion took them home.

NIKITA JEROFEJEVS (6)

QUEEN ELEANOR PRIMARY SCHOOL, NORTHAMPTON

MANUEL'S JUNGLE STORY

One day, Casey and Tom arrived at the scary, scary jungle.
They saw a bad snake. It was slimy.
It wanted to eat them. It hissed. 'Argh!' they shouted.
They saw a kind lion.
The lion said, 'You can climb on my back.'
They went back home. They lived happily ever after.

MANUEL GYAN (5)

QUEEN ELEANOR PRIMARY SCHOOL, NORTHAMPTON

ALYSSA'S JUNGLE STORY

One day, Casey and Tom swung through the dark, scary jungle.
They met a snake. He looked friendly.
But he was scary!
They met a lion. He was happy.
He chased the snake.
Then helped Casey and Tom get home.

ALYSSA BRANNIGAN (6)

QUEEN ELEANOR PRIMARY SCHOOL, NORTHAMPTON

SAMEEHA'S JUNGLE STORY

Once upon a time, there was a girl and a boy called Casey and Tom. Tom and Casey swung in the jungle. They saw a snake, a mean snake. The snake was scary and evil. The children were scared and the snake ran away.

Then they saw a nice lion.

The lion said, 'Hop on my back.'

They swung home.

SAMEEHA RAHMAN (5)
QUEEN ELEANOR PRIMARY SCHOOL, NORTHAMPTON

ZOFIA'S JUNGLE STORY

One day, Casey and Tom went to the jungle.
They saw a snake. Casey screamed.
They ran away.
They saw a friendly lion peeping through the grass.
The lion ran with the children.
The lion took them home. They were happy.

ZOFIA DAROCHA (5)

QUEEN ELEANOR PRIMARY SCHOOL, NORTHAMPTON

JAI-JAI'S JUNGLE STORY

One day, Casey and Tom arrived at the spooky jungle.

Then they saw a snake, it did not look friendly.

They were very frightened. The snake was slimy.

Then they met a friendly lion. The lion said, 'Jump on my back.'

Then they ran away.

They lived happily ever after.

JAI-JAI WEIR (5)

QUEEN ELEANOR PRIMARY SCHOOL, NORTHAMPTON

LIAM'S JUNGLE STORY

There were scary eyes in the jungle. Casey and Tom were scared.
They saw a snake. The snake was long.
The snake was nasty like a vampire.
A lion appeared.
He chase the snake away.
The lion took the children home.

LIAM TURVEY (5)

QUEEN ELEANOR PRIMARY SCHOOL, NORTHAMPTON

Thomas' Jungle Story

Casey and Tom saw a jungle. They were scared of the dark.
They met a snake. It had a smiley face and looked nice.
Then the snake looked like a vampire.
They met a happy lion.
The lion ran away from the snake.
The lion found a house. They were safe.

Thomas Hopper (5)

Queen Eleanor Primary School, Northampton

STAS' JUNGLE STORY

Casey and Tom went to the jungle.
They saw a snake.
The snake hissed. Casey and Tom got scared.
They saw a lion and jumped on his back.
The lion ran away from the snake.
The lion saw the children's house and took them home.

STAS UZORS (6)

QUEEN ELEANOR PRIMARY SCHOOL, NORTHAMPTON

SCARLOTTE'S JUNGLE STORY

One day, Casey and Tom arrived at a creepy jungle. They were scared. They called, 'Help!' but no one came to them.

They saw a creepy snake. They were scared of the snake. They ran round and round but the snake kept on following Casey and Tom. They ran away from the snake.

Tom and Casey met a lion. He helped them escape from the snake. The lion said, 'Hop on my back. Here you go,' said the lion with a smile. 'You're home.'

SCARLOTTE ROSE WILSON-PICKERING (5)

QUEEN ELEANOR PRIMARY SCHOOL, NORTHAMPTON

ELTON'S JUNGLE STORY

One day, Casey and Tom arrived in the jungle.
They saw a naughty snake.
The snake got angry.
The children saw a friendly lion.
The lion took the children home.
The children were happy.

ELTON RAMA (5)

QUEEN ELEANOR PRIMARY SCHOOL, NORTHAMPTON

MASON'S JUNGLE STORY

Tom and Casey went into the deep, dark jungle with scary noises.
They saw an anaconda. Tom and Casey thought the anaconda was nice.
Then the anaconda was not nice. The anaconda was very scary.
Tom and Casey saw a friendly lion. He was very nice to other people.
The lion said, 'Would you like to have a little ride?'
They swung home safely.

MASON WEBB (6)
QUEEN ELEANOR PRIMARY SCHOOL, NORTHAMPTON

HUBERT'S JUNGLE STORY

Casey and Tom went to the jungle. It was scary!
They saw a big yellow snake in the tree.
He was hungry. He chased Casey and Tom. They screamed and ran away.
They saw a happy lion.
He ran after the snake.
He took them home.

HUBERT PIETRZAK (5)
QUEEN ELEANOR PRIMARY SCHOOL, NORTHAMPTON

CHANECIA'S JUNGLE STORY

Once there was a girl called Millie walking in the jungle. She looked around and saw eyes looking at her then Millie climbed up the tree. She saw a snake looking at her, she walked backwards and fell down. Millie landed with a thump.

The snake came down and opened its mouth with its sharp teeth and long tongue. 'Yum, yum!'

This lion, called Mr Jamie, hopped out. It saw the snake and heard Millie scream, 'Help, help!'

He did not like Millie screaming help but he wondered why she needed help, then he ran and ran.

He helped Millie and he took her home.

CHANECIA MORGAN (6)
QUEEN ELEANOR PRIMARY SCHOOL, NORTHAMPTON

JABED'S JUNGLE STORY

One day, a boy flew into space. The rocket was going fast.
He went from Earth, stars were sparkling everywhere. Then the rocket broke and one piece fell down.
Then a spaceship came. It looked friendly.
An alien came out. 'Hello, my name is O. Where have you come from?'
Then the alien helped the boy lift the rocket up and then he took it to Earth.
He took the boy back home and he landed near his house.

JABED ALI (6)
QUEEN ELEANOR PRIMARY SCHOOL, NORTHAMPTON

MILLIE'S JUNGLE STORY

Once upon a time, there lived a boy called Ralph and a girl called Anne. Ralph ran to Anne but Anne was gone. Horrified, he carried on. Just then he remembered that Anne was indestructible.

The next day, she was still not there. Only there was a hissing, scary, giant snake. He shouted, 'Anne!' There was no reply. He was thinking, *I'm going to die!'*

Ralph realised it was a python, he screamed like a girl. You could see the look of hunger in the snake's eyes. Ralph knew who was next. Or did he?

A big lion pounced out of nowhere and the python slithered as quick as a flash back to his home.

'Hey Ralph,' said Anne.

Ralph replied, 'Anne!' As Anne and Ralph walked to somewhere safe the sandal on Ralph's foot fell off but then he picked it up and made a leaf protector so insects didn't eat the leaves.

Anne said, 'Bye.'

Ralph said, 'So you're not my sister!'

'No,' said Anne, 'but we can live together.'

MILLIE DRAINE (7)
QUEEN ELEANOR PRIMARY SCHOOL, NORTHAMPTON

146

MEJA'S UNDER THE SEA STORY

Once upon a time, there was a little girl who was a mermaid called Mrs McMahon. She was a teacher but the classroom had been crashed. She fell in the sea.

She saw a crab, a Nemo fish and all kinds of sea animals. A big animal came along but it wasn't her friend. 'It is just a shark,' she said. It wasn't, it had sharp teeth and it was creepy, it was a shark. 'Oh no,' she said, 'it's getting near me help, help.' She cried as she shouted, 'It's going to eat me, don't, I'm just a little girl, be friendly.' She wobbled her lips as she talked.

Suddenly, her old father appeared from the palace. Her father pointed his magical, powerful stick. The shark was scared of him because he was powerful.

Mrs McMahon was pleased so she gave her daddy a kiss. She danced and danced and danced. She couldn't stop cheering. She said, 'Please Father, can I go out of the sea please?'

'Yes.' She was pleased and her father said, 'Tomorrow it's your birthday, we will have a party today.'

'Thanks Father.'

'You're welcome.'

MEJA ANDRIUKEVIEULE (6)
QUEEN ELEANOR PRIMARY SCHOOL, NORTHAMPTON

Amber's Under The Sea Story

Once upon a time, there were two people called Amber and Joyce. Joyce was Amber's best friend.

Suddenly, they fell underwater and a crab appeared out of nowhere. The crab said, 'Hello, what's your name?'

'Amber, and this is Joyce,' replied Amber.

Suddenly, a great white shark appeared. Joyce and Amber swam as fast as their little jelly legs could carry them.

Then a mermaid appeared and scared the shark away. The mermaid's name was Jenna.

Jenna and her father were very happy. The father and Jenna led them back to the boat.

Jenna, her father, Amber and Joyce lived happily ever after.

Amber Lineham (7)
Queen Eleanor Primary School, Northampton

MYSHA'S SPACE STORY

One day, a rocket came to Earth. Louis was doing his homework outside in his tent, when the rocket landed on Louis' house.

The aliens got out of the rocket and took Louis and he did his homework in the ship.

Louis looked out of the window and he saw stars brighter than the sun and he saw all the different planets.

When he got there a big alien with three eyes jumped in front of Louis and said, 'Hello.'

The aliens took Louis for a cup of tea, when he'd finished his cup of tea he said bye.

They then took Louis back home and gave him his homework back. Louis ran inside and told his mum.

MYSHA AHMAD (7)
QUEEN ELEANOR PRIMARY SCHOOL, NORTHAMPTON

MAX'S SPACE STORY

I was flying to the moon. I wanted to go faster so I pressed the button.

I was nearly there but I went past it so I pressed the slow button then I got on the moon.

I saw an alien's ship flying to the moon too so I stopped and thought, *why is there an alien ship landing on the moon?*

I took a picture of the alien but my rocket broke down. 'How about I help you?' said the nice alien.

He took me home. He was going fast. He went fast so he got home quicker. I got home safely. I gave him a present, it was a helmet.

MAX SNOW (7)
QUEEN ELEANOR PRIMARY SCHOOL, NORTHAMPTON

MATTHEW'S SPACE STORY

Once an orange spaceship flew to the moon and it was really dark. Next the rocket lost one of its bits and then the rocket couldn't get any more power.

After, the rocket crash-landed on the moon. They could see the whole world and next to them was the bit that fell off.

A strange thing happened, a spaceship landed next to them. All the lights flashed. The people in the orange rocket recognised it, some strange lights were underneath.

Then an alien came and said, 'Can I help you? What do you need help with?'

'Yes a bit has broken off our rocket and we can't fix it.'

Then in one minute it was fixed and the spaceship flew away. It took a long time to get home.

Then they were home and their mum was so pleased.

MATTHEW YATES (7)
RED HILL FIELD PRIMARY SCHOOL, LEICESTER

OWEN'S UNDER THE SEA STORY

The people who were in this boat have drowned!
A crab came out of its shell and crawled along the seabed.
The crab jumped into its shell because he saw a terrifying shark!
A mermaid saved the crab and got rid of the shark.
'Thank you,' said the crab.
'My pleasure,' said the mermaid.
So they all went to see the lost boat.

OWEN GRASSBY (6)
RED HILL FIELD PRIMARY SCHOOL, LEICESTER

ETHAN'S JUNGLE STORY

In the jungle I saw 26 staring eyes looking at me. It looked terrifying and it looked nasty.

I saw a snake on a tree, it looked horrible.

But when it turned round it pulled a terrifying face at me.

I saw something moving. I did not know what it was. I was frightened. It was a lion. I ran back home and went straight up to my bedroom. When I looked out of my window the lion was still there.

ETHAN MAISTO (6)

RED HILL FIELD PRIMARY SCHOOL, LEICESTER

POPPIE'S MAGICAL STORY

One summer's morning, a bright rainbow appeared over the gleaming castle and then a dragon appeared at the castle gate.

The dragon roared at the castle gate and roared again. Then the castle guards came running out of the castle gates and saw the dragon, it was huge.

The terrifying dragon roared really loud and it scared the knights away because the roar was really loud.

Then a unicorn came but the unicorn was not the only one who was in the woods. There was a witch hiding behind the tree.

The witch said to her broomstick, 'Look over there, there's my unicorn, I've been looking for it everywhere.'

She captured the unicorn and went home. She cooked the unicorn and ate the unicorn up.

POPPIE HOSEASON (6)
RED HILL FIELD PRIMARY SCHOOL, LEICESTER

SPENCER'S SPACE STORY

A space rocket went to the moon.
It landed on the moon. Something broke off the rocket.
A saucer came to the rocket.
An alien came out of the saucer.
The saucer picked the rocket up.
The saucer put the rocket down on the ground.

SPENCER PHILLIPS (6)
RED HILL FIELD PRIMARY SCHOOL, LEICESTER

AARON'S DINOSAUR STORY

One sunny day a man called John was going inside a time machine. John pressed a button.

It took John to a land. It was full of dinosaurs! John saw a friendly stegosaurus, it was walking up the hill.

When the stegosaurus was on top of the hill, a T-rex was charging from the bush to chase the stegosaurus.

When the T-rex stopped and had a rest, it saw a nest. The T-rex was trying to get the nest but it was too high.

Suddenly... a pterodactyl was in the sky, it was heading to the nest! It saw the T-rex and stuck the T-rex to his leg and dropped him to the river.

John had to go now so he went inside the time machine and pressed the button. It took him back home.

AARON CHEN (6)

RED HILL FIELD PRIMARY SCHOOL, LEICESTER

STAN'S MAGICAL STORY

One day, there was a castle where nobody went.

There was a fierce dragon on the muddy hill.

One evening there was a battle. The dragon was howling out fire because he wanted to kill the unicorn.

'Now the sizzling battle that we've all been waiting for, who will win?' said the dragon.

The witch was flying on her powerful broom. Suddenly her broom was too fast but she had an idea so she jumped.

The witch fell in the tree. She had an idea again, her idea was to kick the broom and she did but it fell in the tree.

STAN ENGLISH (5)

RED HILL FIELD PRIMARY SCHOOL, LEICESTER

EMILY'S UNDER THE SEA STORY

Once upon a time, lived a king and a princess. One day, they decided to go in the sea. They took a boat and then jumped into the sea and turned into mermaids.

The king and princess turned into the King and Princess of the Sea, also all the animals in the sea danced for them.

Then a shark came and frightened the sea animals away. The King and the Princess of the Sea were very cross.

The King and the Princess of the Sea frightened the shark away and they never saw the shark again.

Every sea animal cheered so loud. They cheered until they were out of breath.

Everyone said, 'Bye-bye.' After that they went home and the King and the Princess of the Sea turned back into the King and Princess of the Land.

EMILY BARR (7)
RED HILL FIELD PRIMARY SCHOOL, LEICESTER

FATIMA'S MAGICAL STORY

Once upon a time, there lived a castle. The castle was massive.

In the castle there was a dragon, the dragon was fierce. He had long wings. After that he trotted across the hard floor.

The fierce dragon stuck his tongue out, fire came out of his mouth because he was angry!

The dragon saw a horse. The horse looked helpful and sensible. The dragon fiercely got his claws out.

There was a witch who looked nice. She had a witch's hat and she had something in her hand, it was a silly broom!

After that, the silly broom saw a house, a little house with a moon on top. The moon was asleep, everyone was.

FATIMA SANYANG (7)

RED HILL FIELD PRIMARY SCHOOL, LEICESTER

EMILE'S DINOSAUR STORY

I adventured to the dinosaurs and saw a tyrannosaurus!
I saw lava coming from a volcano.
A velociraptor appeared.
He had horns on his back.
A dinosaur landed on a cloud.
I landed in my garden.

EMILE VERNON (6)
RED HILL FIELD PRIMARY SCHOOL, LEICESTER

OWAIN'S JUNGLE STORY

A gloomy, dark jungle with loads of eyes and spooky, spooky, horrible sounds.

Sssss, a python appeared, It was alone in the jungle but every time a bug went near it it opened its mouth.

A king cobra wanted to eat the python

A lion appeared out of the leaves and saved the python but the cobra spit venom at the python and the python died.

The lion was cross and defeated the cobra. He was not about to get up, the cobra was buried in the sand and went to Heaven.

OWAIN RAFFERTY (5)
RED HILL FIELD PRIMARY SCHOOL, LEICESTER

FINLEY'S SPACE STORY

Once upon a time, there lived a little boy called Sam. He wanted to be an astronaut when he was older.

10 years later he was 20. It was his first time in space. He got into his rocket and the rocket zoomed off into space. He was near Mars.

He saw a flying saucer, it was coming towards him. He was scared.

The alien was scary.

The saucer took the ship.

It took the ship home.

FINLEY GAMBLE (7)
RED HILL FIELD PRIMARY SCHOOL, LEICESTER

FRANCESCA'S DINOSAUR STORY

Once upon a time, there were two people and we made a time machine, it took us to the Land of Dinosaurs.

When we got there we saw a Puertasaurus and a volcano, it erupted...

But after that the huge T-rex came along and it tried to chase us and it nearly ate us.

Now we had found the eggs. 'We can take them.'

'No we can't, do you know why? Because the mummy's coming, run!'

The mummy was right above us. 'Keep going before she gets us. Quick, get to the time machine.'

We were there. 'Now get in the time machine.' We were back home.

FRANCESCA VICTORIA BOWEN (7)

RED HILL FIELD PRIMARY SCHOOL, LEICESTER

JOSHUA'S JUNGLE STORY

One gloomy night in the forest, a snake called Slither loved adventures.
Then suddenly he saw a tree, he was excited.
Suddenly, the king of the cobras came, he jumped. Slither was terrified.
Then a lion came. The cobra was terrified. He tried to get away.
The lion chased the cobra but he was too slow.
The lion took a breath then he ran to a house.

JOSHUA MICHAEL HALL (5)
RED HILL FIELD PRIMARY SCHOOL, LEICESTER

SHRIYA'S MAGICAL STORY

Once upon a time, there lived a princess, a queen, a king and a prince.
They lived in a castle, a castle of rainbows, but something happened.
A fierce dragon came. 'Oh no!' said the princess.
'No fear,' said the prince. 'I shall slay the dragon.'
The dragon breathed fire. The prince and his horse fought the dragon.
It burnt down the castle. 'Oh my!' said the queen. 'What are we going
to do?' The prince tried his best.
The dragon nearly ate the unicorn! The prince said, 'Stay away
from the unicorn.' The dragon flew away from the unicorn, but then
somebody came.
A fairy godmother helped them. The dragon was slain.
They lived happily ever after.

SHRIYA KAUR SUWALI (6)
RED HILL FIELD PRIMARY SCHOOL, LEICESTER

OLIVIA'S SPACE STORY

A boy called Calum was building a red rocket. When his mum, dad and sister were asleep, his rocket took off into space. He could see Earth. He was going to crash on an alien planet. It was dark.

He saw a space thing so he was scared of it. Calum was very scared indeed.

He met an alien girl. She was called Scarlett. She was mad because she thought he was a ghost.

Something took his red rocket away when he was having lunch inside it. Why did they do that?

It took him back home because he was scared of everything in Alien Land World.

OLIVIA JACQUES (7)
RED HILL FIELD PRIMARY SCHOOL, LEICESTER

SCARLETT'S SPACE STORY

A girl called Violet had a yellow space rocket. She was going to space while her family were asleep. Her rocket blasted off to Planet Alien. She saw the world. She said, 'It is amazing.' She was going to crash land. She saw a thing on Planet Alien and something came out of it. She didn't know what it was. She said, 'Who are you?'

The thing said, 'I am an alien and my name is Blob.'

'Blob?' she said. 'That is a funny name.'

'That thing you saw was my spaceship. I am a boy, do you know?'

The alien's spaceship was scanning the rocket. Violet said, 'It is getting dark now so I will go home, see you tomorrow.'

The alien's spaceship took Violet home.

SCARLETT TUCKER (7)
RED HILL FIELD PRIMARY SCHOOL, LEICESTER

MARK'S DINOSAUR STORY

I built a massive time machine and it took me 100,000 years ago. There was a volcano and there was a stegosaurus and a diplodocus. I heard the exploding volcano. Then I went to a gloomy jungle. I wandered into the jungle.

Then... a tyrannosaurus rex came out of nowhere. I tripped the dinosaur up, the tyrannosaurus was trampled on as a pterodactyl stampede began!

In one tree there was a pterodactyl nest. The eggs were hatching. Their mother was trapped then she flew up to a cloud to see the nest. She flew down to the nest. The eggs weren't harmed.

Then the time machine took me home and when my mum called me for tea she did not know I had been 100,000 years ago. I had sandwiches.

MARK NASH (5)
RED HILL FIELD PRIMARY SCHOOL, LEICESTER

OLIVER'S JUNGLE STORY

A gloomy, dark jungle with loads of eyes and spooky, spooky horrible sounds.

A *ssssss* and a python appeared.

It was alone in the jungle but a king cobra wanted to eat the python.

A lion peered out of the leaves and saved the python.

The cobra spat venom at the python. The python died.

The lion was cross and defeated the cobra.

OLIVER DUNK (6)

RED HILL FIELD PRIMARY SCHOOL, LEICESTER

Tia's Magical Story

Once upon a time, there lived a beautiful princess in a glamorous castle and she had a visitor, he was very handsome.

When the princess looked out the window there was a boy frightening a dragon. The princess said, 'Hide!'

The dragon sniffed but he couldn't see them. The fire-breathing dragon was looking around her.

Her flying unicorn saved them.

Tia Bell (6)
Red Hill Field Primary School, Leicester

170

ETHAN'S JUNGLE STORY

Once upon a time, Liam and I went to a jungle. The jungle was dark and gloomy!
We could see plants, long grass and snakes! Liam had glasses, I had blue eyes.
In the jungle we saw a cobra, python and an adder.
Liam wandered off to explore. Where could he be?
Liam shouted, 'I've found him!'

ETHAN POTTER (6)
RED HILL FIELD PRIMARY SCHOOL, LEICESTER

DAISIE'S UNDER THE SEA STORY

Daisie and Lilly were friends. They both wanted to see what it's like under the water but the next minute they both were under the water. They didn't know how they got under the water.

When they were swimming in the sea Daisie was caught by lots and lots of seaweed at the bottom of the dark, dark sea. Lilly pulled and pulled but she didn't come free. She pulled and pulled again but this time she was free!

At last Daisie and Lilly found the king whale, they were happy.

DAISIE TOMPSETT (6)
RED HILL FIELD PRIMARY SCHOOL, LEICESTER

OM'S SPACE STORY

Once upon a time, Max woke up, he put his clothes on because it was the day he had to go to space! He ran outside. He went inside his rocket, pressed the blast-off button, the rocket went to space.
He landed his rocket. He looked outside. He was on a planet.
Then there was a saucer. Max went out of his rocket, he saw the aliens!
He went back in his rocket and he was safe.

OM CHAUHAN (6)
RED HILL FIELD PRIMARY SCHOOL, LEICESTER

WILLIAM'S UNDER THE SEA STORY

One bright day, Sam and Max went fishing on their boat. Then a shark tipped the boat over.

They swam around the sea. When they stopped they saw a rainbowfish. They saw its shiny scales.

They swam past it, then they saw a shark. They hid in the seaweed. It passed. Finally it was gone. It swam through the seaweed.

WILLIAM PRIESTLEY (6)

RED HILL FIELD PRIMARY SCHOOL, LEICESTER

ZARA'S UNDER THE SEA STORY

Ariel was unhappy. Suddenly... Tangled leapt into the water.
Today Ariel was going to have tea with Prince Eric but she couldn't say no to playing with Tangled so, as she couldn't decide, she did both.
Finally, Ariel was happy. It was time to go.
They all said goodbye. Suddenly... King Triton and Sebastian told Ariel off...
Then they all lived happily ever after.

ZARA SURA-ROBERTS (6)
RED HILL FIELD PRIMARY SCHOOL, LEICESTER

CHLOE'S JUNGLE STORY

One sunny afternoon, Biff, Chip and Kipper were in Biff's room when the magic key began to glow. It took them to a jungle!
There were two monkeys and one elephant. Suddenly, they saw four nasty snakes! The snakes began to chase after them, but then the magic key began to glow so that meant it was time for Biff, Chip and Kipper to go home!

CHLOE MELISSA TROWN (7)
RED HILL FIELD PRIMARY SCHOOL, LEICESTER

POPPY'S UNDER THE SEA STORY

One sunny morning, Rose and Grace woke up and for their breakfast they had egg and bacon sandwiches.

They went to a beach and they jumped in the water and they turned into mermaids.

They found a deep, dark, gloomy cave and then a bad mermaid came out. Grace and Rose were terrified.

Then the King of the Ocean came and the bad mermaid got put in a cage.

They had a party. Rose was pleased. Grace and Rose went back home and had tea. For tea they had fish and chips and then it was time for bed. Grace said, 'Tea was nice.'

POPPY JASPER (7)
RED HILL FIELD PRIMARY SCHOOL, LEICESTER

JAMES' MAGICAL STORY

Once upon a time, there was a castle in a magical land called Happy Land.

There was a dragon called Toothy passing by about to breathe out his fire. He changed his colour from red to green so he could be in camouflage.

Oh no! Toothy let out his fire! What was going to happen? Would Happy Land turn into Sad Land? Who is going to save the day?

Then a unicorn appeared and Toothy suddenly stopped breathing his fire and he fell in love with the unicorn!

A witch (who was a good witch) had put a spell on Toothy using her broomstick to make him fall in love. How clever.

The broomstick went home to the witch's pink house. The moon came up then everyone lived happily ever after.

JAMES HOOSON (6)
ST MARY'S CE PRIMARY SCHOOL, HINCKLEY

FREYA'S MAGICAL STORY

There was once a magical kingdom called The Land of Frey. In that kingdom there was Princess Freya who was a very nice and kind princess. Her best friends were Prince James and Prince Corey.
The three of them would always be going out on adventures in the forest behind the kingdom.
In the forest they say a big scary dragon lives there. When they came across the dragon he looked scary and dangerous because he breathed fire.
Princess Freya had a magical unicorn. The unicorn used its magical powers and quickly befriended the dragon.
On one of their other adventures they came across an evil witch called Gertrude the Horrible. Gertrude tried to use her spells against them to turn them into monkeys but it didn't work, as princess Freya used her unicorn to turn Gertrude into a rat.
They then used her broomstick to fly back to the kingdom.

FREYA JOANNE PACKER (6)
ST MARY'S CE PRIMARY SCHOOL, HINCKLEY

ALIEN MONSTERS

Once there were ten alien monster friends called Bill, Ben, Max, John, Curtis, Ellie, Daisy, Poppy, Annabelle and Bella. They had three eyes, two on the top of their stalks and one in their forehead. They had two fingers on their left hand, seven on the right. They had blue and purple skin, 10 legs and they lived on Planet Bong.

It was extremely cold on Planet Bong and they got very cold toes! So Ben looked at Planet Draw in his telescope to see how they kept warm, but the aliens didn't have any feet - so that was no help.

Next Ellie looked in her telescope at Planet Gleab. Planet Gleab was a very hot planet, so that did not help.

Curtis looked at Planet Mashbean in his telescope, but all of the aliens were on holiday. Then Bill had an idea! He had heard of a planet that was hot in some places but cold in others! The aliens on this planet had feet and went on holiday in their own world. The planet was called Earth! The alien monsters jumped into their spaceship and blasted off to Earth. Poppy was scared and as soon as they landed she kissed the ground. They looked up from where they had landed and saw lots of children playing football.

They all had long, warm, woolly socks on their feet. Bella had a plan. She told Max and Ben to hide in the laundry basket so when the children took off their socks they could grab them!

Max and Ben weren't gone long, they were soon back with lots of warm, woolly, long socks! John told everyone to get back into the

spaceship and off they zoomed.

When they got home, they unpacked the socks which smelt like cheese and gave them to Annabelle to wash. They never had cold feet again.

LILLY ANNE DUNMORE (6)

ST MARY'S CE PRIMARY SCHOOL, HINCKLEY

UNTITLED

On a cold, misty morning, a little boy called Stanley was woken up by his daddy shouting, 'Wake up, get ready.'

That morning, Stanley was going to help his daddy build their new house. Stanley jumped up, got dressed and raced downstairs. He had breakfast and went outside where his dad was cutting wood. 'What can I do Dad?'

'You can do this.' Stanley's dad handed him a saw. Stanley knew he had to be very careful.

He spent the day sawing and collecting materials on his quad bike. 'Well done Stanley!'

STANLEY SMITH (7)
ST MARY'S CE PRIMARY SCHOOL, HINCKLEY

BERTIE

There was a dog named Bertie, his owners left him in a field by accident and then he smelt all the things he liked. He ran and next he met some people who were having a picnic, he played football with them.

Then they read his collar and it said: '12 Gilbert Street', so he ran home as fast as he could, his owners were happy.

DANIEL LEATHER (6)
ST MARY'S CE PRIMARY SCHOOL, HINCKLEY

THE MAGIC FAIRY BALLERINA SAVES THE DAY!

Once upon a time, there was a magical fairy ballerina called Amber. One day, Amber had just finished her ballet recital and she was riding her pet unicorn called Daisy home. All of a sudden, Amber's wings started to glow bright pink. She was very scared, it had never happened before. 'What's the matter?' cried Amber. Amber rode Daisy to the fairy king and queen to see if they could tell her why her wings were glowing.

They told her that a little girl called Holly needed help with her ballet because she is not very good at it. So Amber waved her wand and suddenly she was in the humans' world.

'There are lots of people. They are very big,' Amber said. Then she saw Holly. Amber knew it was Holly because she had a picture of her. The king and queen had given it to her. She then saw Holly practising her ballet with her friend but she did everything wrong. Amber walked towards Holly and said, 'Hello.'

Holly said, 'Hello,' too.

'I am going to teach you some ballet steps,' Amber said.

'Thank you very much,' said Holly.

After Amber had taught Holly some steps Holly said, 'Let's do a ballet recital.' So Holly and her friend, Sophie, put on a ballet show.

'It is fabulous,' said Amber.

Holly and Sophie got a standing ovation.

After that Amber had to go back to Fairy Land so she waved goodbye and waved her wand and she was back in Fairy Land. She went to her home, got her pyjamas and read her book. She watched a bit of TV, then fed her pet unicorn. She had a drink of milk and a biscuit and then fell fast asleep.

MADISON WILCOX (7)
ST MARY'S CE PRIMARY SCHOOL, HINCKLEY

UNTITLED

In the sisters' house it was bedtime. Rachel and her sister, Kirsty were getting ready for bed. Rachel and Kirsty had a special secret, they were friends with the fairy princess. They got into their beds and fell fast asleep. Just at that moment, something began to glow and woke the two sisters up. Then a light carried them all the way to Fairy Land. 'Kirsty, Rachel, I'm so glad you're here, the naughty goblins have taken our dancing liquid,' Ruby said.

'We must find it!' Rachel said. 'Let's go, up on top of that hill is the goblins' castle.'

They got to the castle, they had to be very quiet so the goblins couldn't hear them. They crept in and looked at the really big cupboard, written on it was a sign saying: *Things that have been stolen*, but they saw two goblins guarding the door.

Just then Rachel had an idea, she whispered it to Kirsty and Ruby. Ruby shook her wand and sound came out like this, 'Right lads; tea break.' Then the goblins moved and the girls got to go in the cupboard. They got the liquid back and said goodbye to Ruby and set off for home.

'There is the light,' Rachel said. They stepped in and it took them all the way home, straight into their beds.

In the morning, Rachel and Kirsty found some fairy dust and whispered, 'Thank you.'

ROSE FORREST (6)
ST MARY'S CE PRIMARY SCHOOL, HINCKLEY

DINOSAUR TIME

One sunny day in prehistoric times, T-rex and Diplodocus decided to have a football match.

Two hours later kick-off began... 'Dinosaur Diples' vs 'Cavemen Cotters'. It was going well for Dinosaur Diples. Suddenly, Diplodocus headed in a corker. The whistle blew, half-time. 1-0 to Dinosaur Diples.

The second half started. Suddenly, Captain Caveman fouled Allosaurus. Penalty, then Allosaurus took it and scored. Suddenly, the ref blew his whistle, full time. 2-0 to Dinosaur Diples.

After the match they all had a party!

ALFIE STORER (7)
ST MARY'S CE PRIMARY SCHOOL, HINCKLEY

ROSE AND HER SISTER SAVE THE DAY

It was a rainy, horrible, grey day when Rose and Daisy were bored and they didn't know what to do. Their mother said, 'How about you go swimming?' Daisy, the bigger sister wanted to go swimming so they got their things ready.

When they arrived they saw a man with a dog. He didn't follow the rules because the sign on the wall said: *No Dogs Allowed*, he looked at the sign and ignored it. He took the dog off the lead and the dog Alix jumped in the water and the man left his dog drowning. But Rose and Daisy were good swimmers so they dived for the dog.

When they got him they got the police and they put the man in prison. The keeper of the swimming pool said, 'You can come here whenever you want to and you can come for free.'

They went home and told their mother and father all about it and they were surprised. They said, 'You can do anything you want at home and you can have two puddings after your dinner.' They went trick or treating because it was Halloween and they stayed up till half past midnight.

Then they went to bed.

AIMEE FRASER (5)
ST MARY'S CE PRIMARY SCHOOL, HINCKLEY

APPLE TREE FARM

On a tall, dark, misty hill there was a spooky, stinky, dark farm. It was called Apple Tree Farm. On the farm lived a tall man called Fred and a small lady called Polly. They had a daughter called Chloe. She was tall too, just like her dad. Her hair was really long and black. She was nine years old and loved reading about vampires, also witches. The family were very poor. They had to share just one bed and had no bath to wash in. The farm was really dirty and it had no animals left.

Chloe's mum and dad were scared of everything, but Chloe was a brave girl.

At night on the farm, Chloe would hear mooing noises and she wished she had lots of animals on her farm so her family could be rich.

One night, a little girl vampire came into Chloe's room. Her name was Sarah and she was a kind vampire. Sarah and Chloe played lots of games and became best friends.

In the morning the sparkly sun was coming up and it was time for Sarah to go home. Before she went she could give Chloe a wish. Chloe wished for the farm to be better! Sarah made the wish come true. Chloe went to sleep. When she woke up she heard mooing, oinking, quacking, baaing and cock-a-doodle-dooing. Their farm was brilliant. Chloe and her mum and dad were rich. All of the people in the village said, 'They are rich! Rich! Rich!'

Sarah the vampire always still came to Apple Tree Farm every Friday night to play games and see the animals with her best friend, Chloe.

Lucy Edlin-Gill (6)
St Mary's CE Primary School, Hinckley

STANLEY'S DINOSAUR STORY

One morning, a little boy found a spaceship, he went in and pulled a lever. The spaceship burst into life.

The spaceship landed on a dinosaur island. The boy opened the door.

A nasty dinosaur tried to eat him but he threw a stone at his eye and he ran off.

The boy climbed up a tree. He saw three eggs. He knocked one off, it fell out of the tree, it cracked.

The mummy came back, she was cross. She grabbed the boy but the boy managed to escape.

He ran as fast as he could to get back to the spaceship. He pulled the lever and zoomed home and he told his mum about it.

STANLEY NEALE (7)
ST MARY'S CE PRIMARY SCHOOL, HINCKLEY

LACEY-AVA'S MAGICAL STORY

Princess Jasmine lived in a beautiful blue castle.

One day, along came a green dragon. He tried to eat the princess. The dragon could breathe fire.

The dragon also tried to eat the princess' unicorn.

A friendly witch cast a spell to make the dragon go away and she saved the princess.

After saving the princess the witch went home to her yellow house with her broomstick.

LACEY-AVA SIMMONS (5)

ST MARY'S CE PRIMARY SCHOOL, HINCKLEY

SUKI'S MAGICAL STORY

Once there was a princess who lived in a castle, she had blonde hair. Her job was to look after children. The princess played games with the children.

Along came a nice dragon called Ben. He wanted to play with them, but he had never ever had friends so he did not know how to play. He thought that breathing fire was fun! But it scared the princess and the children. They showed Ben how to play fun games like hide-and-seek.

While playing hide-and-seek, Ben the dragon met a unicorn called Alice. She had blue fur and was known for not being very nice.

Alice told the witch how to find the children. However, it was a very nice witch. She gave a magic wand to the dragon. He used two wishes. First he wished for a house to give to the children. Secondly he wished for Alice to be a nice unicorn.

The children and Alice lived happily ever after.

SUKI CHEN (5)
ST MARY'S CE PRIMARY SCHOOL, HINCKLEY

CALUM'S JUNGLE STORY

In the gloomy woods, there were some scary eyes. It was some snakes staring at a little boy. The boy was lost and sad because his house was on fire.

Suddenly, a slithery snake jumped out of a bush and bit the little boy, who screamed!

Meanwhile, on the other side of the woods, a cute lion was minding his own business until he heard a scream. The lion looked in the swishy bushes, he looked in the swishy grass and he looked in the swishy trees, but the scream wasn't there.

The lion ran as fast as he could until he found the boy. He pounced and he killed the scary snake.

The friendly lion showed the boy the way to a new home.

CALUM THOMAS DAWKINS (5)
ST MARY'S CE PRIMARY SCHOOL, HINCKLEY

LUIS' JUNGLE STORY

Once upon a time in a forest, lived 13 bats. The branches in the forest were magic.

The friendly snake lived in the wild forest with 13 bats. His name was Bob.

One morning, a viper came to the forest and made a lot of hissing.

The lion heard all the noise and wanted to find out what it was!

The lion saw the nasty viper and ran away! The lion ran and ran all the way home.

The lion lived happily ever after.

LUIS ASHBY (6)

ST MARY'S CE PRIMARY SCHOOL, HINCKLEY

KAI'S MAGICAL STORY

Once upon a time, there was a tall, scary castle in Nottingham. The castle had no drawbridge but it had a furious knight. The king gave the knight a mission...

This was to slay the Ender Dragon. The knight died!

The dragon was actually good, he looked at the knight's next mission. This was to save the unicorn and get a clue.

The Ender Dragon saved the unicorn so she gave him a clue. The clue was to get the broomstick to the broom shop, but the broom was on fire.

No worries, the dragon put it out. Then the dragon frozen the witch. The broom got home and they lived happily ever after.

KAI RYAN-EVANS (6)
ST MARY'S CE PRIMARY SCHOOL, HINCKLEY

HARVEY'S UNDER THE SEA STORY

One day two men had diving suits in their boat. They also had air tanks and flippers. The two men had rowed the boat to the middle of the sea. One of the men stood up and dropped the anchor over the side of the boat.

The divers got dressed in their diving suits and carefully got into the sea. The two divers swam under the water. One of the divers had an underwater camera. He took a picture of jellyfish and a baby tiger shark. The other diver called Jack swam to his friend Max. In the distance Jack could just about see an old shipwreck.

The two divers swam towards the old ship. Jack and Max spotted a man who had drowned with his ship. The divers made their way into the captain's quarters and in the corner of the room was a treasure chest. Jack swam back to the drowned man and in his hand was a golden key. Jack swam back to Max with the key and opened the treasure chest.

Jack saw a large fin swim past the hole in the ship. It was a great white shark. The divers were scared and dropped the treasure. The two friends swam towards the surface.

Above them the rowing boat and safety; below, the shark. The divers' air tanks were empty and they were so close to the surface. The two divers dropped their tanks and reached the boat. Still gasping for air, the two divers rowed to shore. There was no sign of the shark and no sign of the treasure. 'We could have been rich!' said Max. Jack felt a sharp pain coming from his wet suit pocket. Thinking it was a rock, he reached in and pulled out a large diamond.

'We are rich!' said Jack.

HARVEY LEE (6)
ST MARY'S CE PRIMARY SCHOOL, HINCKLEY

OLIVIA'S MAGICAL STORY

Once upon a time, there was a castle and a princess. The princess was called Emma.

A dragon came and the dragon's name was Bob. The princess said, 'Dragons are horrible.'

The dragon was breathing fire. He was really mad because he saw a unicorn. He did not like unicorns. He said, 'I don't like unicorns.'

When he saw the unicorn he said, 'Ha ha ha,' to the little unicorn.

The little unicorn said, 'Hi.'

A witch wanted to take the princess' tiara. She said, 'Ha ha ha, I'll get her tiara!'

Suddenly the witch's broom ran away! 'Oh no, my broom! Come back Broom! I'm going home!'

OLIVIA STOKES (6)

THRINGSTONE PRIMARY SCHOOL, COALVILLE

ANGEL'S MAGICAL STORY

On a cold, dark night, a princess was asleep in her tower. When it was morning she had breakfast and she looked out of her window and she saw a dragon!

The dragon breathed fire, the dragon said, 'Ha ha ha ha ha!'

The dragon breathed fire again. The princess said, 'Help, help!' Then a prince saved the princess.

A unicorn came and killed the dragon. Then a witch came. The witch was pretending to be good because she wanted to steal the princess' tiara. She said to her broom, 'Go and get it now!'

So they went to get it, but she looked out of her window and saw them running away, she had had enough of them!

ANGEL FINDLEY (6)

THRINGSTONE PRIMARY SCHOOL, COALVILLE

CALLUM'S UNDER THE SEA STORY

Once upon a time, there was a boat floating at the top of the sea. There was no one on the boat anywhere to be seen.

Under the boat right down at the bottom of the sea, there was a crab. The crab liked the fish who lived with him his whole life.

Suddenly, a shark came. A mermaid and the crab hid in his shell. They were going to King Turtle.

King Turtle tried to shoo the shark away. The shark was scared of the king and swam away.

The mermaid was pleased the king had saved her. The mermaid and the king danced at the bottom of the sea. The king was happy swimming with the beautiful mermaid. They went to the top of the boat. 'Let's go on an adventure,' said the king.

CALLUM SMITH (6)

THRINGSTONE PRIMARY SCHOOL, COALVILLE

EDITH'S MAGICAL STORY

Once upon a time, there was a castle. In the castle there was a princess. She had a stepmother. The princess also had stepsisters, the stepsisters were naughty.

A dragon came, it breathed fire at the princess.

The princess ran and ran, the dragon ran so the princess ran even faster.

Later the dragon stood on a unicorn's foot. The dragon said, 'Sorry.'

A witch came, she had a broom, it had eyes and a mouth.

It ran away to a house. The witch ran after it. They lived happily ever after.

EDITH WATSON (6)
THRINGSTONE PRIMARY SCHOOL, COALVILLE

MACIE'S MAGICAL STORY

Once upon a time, there was a castle. It had a garden and the garden had a tree. There was a rainbow in the garden and some flowers.
There came a dragon who was green and big and had long claws.
He was blowing fire out of his mouth.
Then the dragon saw the unicorn. The unicorn was a girl and was nice.
There was a witch in the forest who lived in a house and the house was small.

MACIE ANN LOUISE SHEPHARD (6)
THRINGSTONE PRIMARY SCHOOL, COALVILLE

OLIVER'S JUNGLE STORY

One day in the jungle, there was a snake called Snakey, he was hungry. He slithered lots of places till at last he found some food. He said, 'A mouse!'

He ate the mouse. He said, 'Yum, yum,' but he was still hungry, so hungry.

Then he saw a lion. The snake said hello to the lion who knew Snakey was hungry. 'Come with me to my home to have a McDonald's. What do you want?'

'I'm not sure!'

'Here is my home. I hope you like my home, it is big,' said the lion. 'Do you want to have a sleepover?'

OLIVER MULHERON (6)
THRINGSTONE PRIMARY SCHOOL, COALVILLE

OLIVER'S SPACE STORY

One day, there were four people in a rocket. The man who was driving the rocket was the boss.

Then they were in space, their names were Jim, Clare, Grace and Oliver.

There was a spaceship, in it was an alien and the alien's name was Bob. The alien had three eyes.

The alien said, 'Hello!' The alien was nice. Oliver, Jim, Clare and Grace liked Bob.

Bob wanted their spaceship because he liked it.

He took the spaceship but my family didn't see it...

OLIVER BLAKE (5)
THRINGSTONE PRIMARY SCHOOL, COALVILLE

MAX'S UNDER THE SEA STORY

Once upon a time, a boat was left in the sea.

Under the sea lived a crab. He was a happy crab and he had lots of friends.

Then a shark came looking for the crab.

Then a mermaid scared the shark away. The shark swam and swam until he was out of breath.

The king mermaid and the other one cheered. Hip hip hooray.

'You saved the crab,' said the king mermaid.

'Yes I did.'

MAX JOHNSON (6)

THRINGSTONE PRIMARY SCHOOL, COALVILLE

EDIE'S MAGICAL STORY

Once upon a time, there was a castle. It had a flag and a princess lived in it.

A dragon came, 'Help!' said the princess, the dragon was breathing fire and the dragon had long claws. The dragon was scary.

It saw a unicorn. 'Help!' said the unicorn. 'The dragon's got me!'

A witch came, she saved the unicorn.

'Thank you,' said the unicorn, 'you saved me.'

The witch's broom found a house, it was a purple house.

They all had lunch then they went to the park and they all had fun.

EDIE HUTCHINSON (5)

THRINGSTONE PRIMARY SCHOOL, COALVILLE

WILLIAM'S SPACE STORY

Once upon a time, there was a rocket. It landed on the moon.
It ran out of petrol and crashed.
A spaceship landed on the moon. It sucked the rocket up.
An alien came out from the spaceship.
The spaceship got the rocket and held it.
It took the rocket home.

WILLIAM CHESTER (5)

THRINGSTONE PRIMARY SCHOOL, COALVILLE

KAI'S SPACE STORY

There was a rocket flying around the planet.

Then it crashed on the planet.

There was an alien on the planet. He said hello to the rocket. Then he saw the stars.

He took the rocket so he could fly the rocket.

Then the alien's ship took it home.

Then the alien ship went home.

KAI GOHIL (6)

THRINGSTONE PRIMARY SCHOOL, COALVILLE

OLIVER'S SPACE STORY

Once upon a time, there was an alien called Bob. He lived in a house, his house was so messy he washed himself with sewer water!

He went in a rocket and he flew.

Suddenly, he crashed. An alien got out of his flying saucer, his name was Tim.

Bob met Tim then they had a fight.

They stopped fighting and Tom fixed Bob's ship and sucked it up with his saucer and took Bob home.

'Are we there yet?'

'Nearly, we just need to go past a few more houses.'

'Now are we?'

'Yes!'

'Whoo!' shouted Bob.

OLIVER PEDEN (6)
THRINGSTONE PRIMARY SCHOOL, COALVILLE

THE HAUNTED HOUSE

Once upon a time, there were three people who lived in India.

One day, their mother-in-law was cooking some nice food, chicken with rice.

The next morning they all woke up. However their house had become haunted. They all said, 'Hello, anybody there?'

'Yeah, yeah, yeah,' shrieked a voice. There was a sudden silence. A ghost stole the baby, it went in the bathroom and ate the baby. All that was left was the baby's bones.

The mother missed her little baby. The ghost returned to the house. The mother said, 'You can eat me.'

The ghost never replied. It never replied because it lost its voice and puked the baby out. The baby came back to life and the family was happy once again.

ZOYA SONEJI (7)
UPLANDS INFANT SCHOOL, LEICESTER

THE TIME MACHINE

Once upon a time on a dull morning, my big 'bossy' brother, Zineddine, and I were awake, then my brother was getting bored. Suddenly, he had an amazing idea! He told me to go to the shed so I said, 'No!'
It was dusty and we saw a time machine which we took carefully back to the house.
My brother and I went inside but when he came out we were in Dino Land! I was scared.
The next day the T-rex angrily stamped on the time machine.
Some cavemen came and the animals too, they started to mind the time machine. We safely and slowly went back home and got into our beds.
After that we were never bored again.

SARAH MAHMOUDI (7)
UPLANDS INFANT SCHOOL, LEICESTER

UNTITLED

One bright morning, there was a girl and boy named Lilly and Peter. Lilly was wearing a pink dress with flowers and white tights, Peter was wearing a blue top and jeans with Nike shoes.

Peter and Lilly jumped in their car and quickly drove down the motorway and reached London, the capital city of England.

They started skipping down the road when suddenly two evil dogs started to chase them. Fortunately, they reached the palace and met the king, queen and princess. The king and queen's palace had 100 rooms and the king and queen gave a tour.

When the tour was done they hopped into the car and they rushed back home and they forgot about the dogs.

MARYAM ANIS (7)
UPLANDS INFANT SCHOOL, LEICESTER

THE QUEENS' DOWNFALL

Once upon a time, lived Sanaa, Zoeya and Maryam, queens of sun, moon and light. They were best friends.

One day in Nioc Land, the three queens were practising spells. They put three grapes on the rabbit's head for a hat. When the rabbit popped up it would be funny. When everyone came the queens started the trick. When the rabbit popped up the three grapes fell right into the queens' mouths. The grapes were poisonous! Lots of thorns grew around them all. They slept for six years.

One day, a prince came and kissed them with dark red lips. Suddenly, their eyes started to open. They could feel evil coming. The sky started lightning. The evil darkness appeared! Everyone in Nice Land vanished and no one never ever came back...

SANAA JOGEE (7)
UPLANDS INFANT SCHOOL, LEICESTER

THE SQUID AND THE DRAGON

One gloomy day, a magical, fast squid that had 20 legs and could breathe on land, and a fierce toxic dragon were fighting in Diamond World. There were lots of crystals and diamonds.

The fierce, toxic, deadly dragon went inside the squid's house and tricked the squid, saying, 'Can I have some tea?' But the squid didn't have any tea so he went to the shops. But the fierce, toxic, deadly dragon blew the squid's house up with a deadly grenade.

When the squid entered the house, it was on fire! Then they used a hose, to put the fire out. They argued for two hours.

They had a fight so they both used their powers. Squid used his stinky breath and the fierce, toxic, deadly dragon used his toxic green fire. It was a tie but they both thought that fighting was silly. So they were friends and lived happily ever after.

RAYHAAN MUSHTAQ SHAIKH (7)
UPLANDS INFANT SCHOOL, LEICESTER

SPINEY'S AWESOME ADVENTURE

One sunny morning, I was practising my wrestling skills in my garden, when suddenly a magic key sent me to the ocean. I saw a dinosaur called a spinosaurus, it looked frightening. But, up above I saw a shark guarding something magnificent. It was a hidden city! The city was filled with remarkable flying fish that were covered in colourful stripes!

The shark saw me and it chased me but just then Spiney the spinosaurus bashed the shark. Then the shark's team chased me and Spiney and I had an idea. He called his friends and they bashed their team and we won. We explored the hidden city. It was remarkable and then Spiney took me home.

MUHAMMAD JET (6)
UPLANDS INFANT SCHOOL, LEICESTER

UNTITLED

One sunny day, I was doing my exercises in my room, but suddenly a gigantic, marvellous rocket appeared in front of me. I went inside and there was a red button that said: 'Do not press!'

I pressed the red button and I launched into deep, dark space, the rocket gave me an astronaut costume so I could breathe and so I didn't get cold in deep, dark space.

I got out and I saw an angry alien running to me, but a friendly alien gave me a strong, shiny, gold shield that could defeat the angry alien! Another bad alien destroyed my rocket but I scared the bad alien and he fell off the Planet Mars!

The friendly alien teleported me back home.

Suddenly I woke up in my wonderful house. 'It was a dream! I need to see if everything is okay.' Dreamily I walked downstairs. 'Everything is OK, yay I am back!'

RICARDS SKABURSKIS (7)
UPLANDS INFANT SCHOOL, LEICESTER

UNTITLED

Long, long ago in the Amazon, there lived a boy called Jon. Everyone liked him except one man. His name was Black Bolt! He was hunting for dinosaurs. Dinosaurs were almost extinct but someone told him there was one more left!

One night Jon was asleep and Black Bolt was awake. Black Bolt was making so much noise. Jon woke up. When Jon was on his way to Black Bolt's tent to complain, Jon saw a dinosaur! Jon took the dinosaur back to his tent. Jon named the dinosaur Vamp because he looked like a vampire.

Vamp started to grow. Jon looked for Vamp's mother, but she was dead! Jon thought, he said to himself, 'I'm going to keep you.' So he did. Tom thought again and he said, 'I'm going to show you to Black Bolt,' so he did!

Jon went to Black Bolt's tent. Black Bolt saw Jon holding a stunning dinosaur! Jon was really happy. Black Bolt pretended to be Jon's friend for two days.

One night, Black Bolt vampnapped Jon's dinosaur! Black Bolt was going to kill Vamp with a chainsaw but Jon heard. Jon saw Black Bolt and chased him into a group of great white sharks and no one ever saw Black Bolt again!

THAFEEM CABBO (7)
UPLANDS INFANT SCHOOL, LEICESTER

UNTITLED

One sunny day, I decided I would have lunch in the park. My mum packed me some lunch, we set off. When we got there my mum sat on the bench and read a book whilst I was sitting on the grass having my lunch.

Then I heard a strange munching sound. It was coming from the bushes. All of a sudden, a tiny head popped out. I heard a voice say, 'Who are you?'

'My name is Lilly, what's your name?'

'Diplodocus.'

'How did you get here?'

'I do not know.'

'Oh OK, I am going to tell my mum I met a diplodocus.'

From then on we played together and went home together.

One morning it was very cold. The diplodocus put on a show just for me. It was a summer show, he was very good at acting. Then that night the diplodocus could not sleep well so I said, 'Let's go outside, OK?'

The next morning, my mum had to ring the zoo and the diplodocus had to go. When the zookeeper came they took the diplodocus home. Whilst they were going I waved goodbye when they went down the street.

AAISHA SIDAT

UPLANDS INFANT SCHOOL, LEICESTER

A PREHISTORIC BIRTHDAY

66 million years ago, there was a triceratops named Nit who weighed seven tonnes and was seven years old and lived happily with his family till his eighth birthday.

When Nit woke up the next morning, he was really excited because it was his birthday and he was eight years old now. He was really happy because there were lots of fun planned.

Nit was so surprised he went mad when he saw what his parents had prepared! There were cakes of different shapes and sizes, there was a barbecue and candyfloss stalls and even a bouncy castle!

When it was time to play, they played pass the parcel and hide-and-seek and it was really fun. Nit hid behind the candyfloss stall and as soon as its owner turned away, with his horns he made a hole in the stall and sneaked the candyfloss in the hole for later. He then went to hide under the stall where he was soon found. So he hid somewhere far away from his party where nobody could find him. He stayed there till night-time and he became really scared so he slept in a bush.

Next morning, he woke to the sound of footsteps, he was terrified! But the footsteps were those of his mum looking for him! From that day on, he never left his herd.

MUHSIN MEEAHKHAN (7)
UPLANDS INFANT SCHOOL, LEICESTER

BAD JELLYFISH

One sunny day, Judy and Peter went to the beach. Peter put his foot inside the water but something was pulling him and it was pink. Judy was sure it was a jellyfish and it was a jellyfish. 'The jellyfish looks beautiful, but they are dangerous,' said Judy.

Then suddenly Peter closed his eyes and did you know that Judy was about to faint? Soon Judy called Mum and Dad and they came straight away.

Peter was about to drown, the jellyfish shot a powerful hole into Peter's body and sadly he had died.

Judy, Mum and Dad felt like hitting and slapping that jellyfish so Dad and Mum had a big stick in their hand and they were hitting the jellyfish so hard that the jellyfish never came back again.

ZAINAB MASTER (7)
UPLANDS INFANT SCHOOL, LEICESTER

UNTITLED

One beautiful sunny day I went in my time machine and I went to the dinosaurs' land.

I saw some scary dinosaurs roaring at me. I ran away.

Then a T-rex came, he wanted to catch me too. So I ran and ran and the T-rex wasn't there.

Next, I found some shiny white eggs and I saw a dinosaur swooping in the sky. It was the mum so I gave her the eggs.

She swooped off with the shiny white eggs and she went back home.

Finally, I got in my time machine and went back home.

LOOAY JOUHARI (6)

UPLANDS INFANT SCHOOL, LEICESTER

UNTITLED

One scorching hot day, I went to a shop. Then I found a time machine and I entered the password. Then I went to the olden days.

I heard a mighty roar. I was frightened. Afterwards, I felt hungry, so hungry! I remembered I had a packed lunch then I ate it all! I was thinking, *am I late for tea?*

I realised I was not so I went to find some food. I saw an enormous dinosaur. It roared, roar! I was terrified.

It disappeared then I thought I saw something, it was an egg! The egg hatched into a baby pterodactyl. Its mum was coming, I went behind a tree.

I saw an apple, I ate it all except the seeds. The dinosaur's mum was landing. I ran away so far I nearly got lost.

I had had enough, time to go home for tea. I ran back to the time machine and went home.

SAIRAH BHAYAT (6)
UPLANDS INFANT SCHOOL, LEICESTER

Asbah And The Dinosaurs

One windy day, I found a time machine that took me back to Dinosaur Land. In Dinosaur Land I saw big leaves swishing. Also I heard some T-rexes stomping because they were angry and fierce.

Suddenly, I got chased by a T-rex. I hid by a cave. I found some eggs and took care of them.

Then a dinosaur came and scooped the eggs up.

I chased the dinosaur but it went up into the cold clouds. 'Oh no!' I said.

But a kind dinosaur let me sit on its back and flew up to the cold clouds and snatched the eggs from me. He took them through the trees and gave them to the mother that had lost the eggs. The mother was so pleased so she gave me the leaves. I loved the leaves.

I went home but the dinosaurs did not want me to go. I said, 'I have to go back to my lovely home.' I waved bye-bye.

I went home and put the leaves in my cupboard.

Asbah Daud (6)
Uplands Infant School, Leicester

MAGIC TIME MACHINE

One sunny day, I went to my colourful time machine and went to Dinosaur Land. Suddenly, I heard a roaring noise. It was a masssive green T-rex! I ran as fast as I could.

At last I lost the T-rex. I was so tired. Suddenly I saw something, there were some little eggs. There were three eggs in total. I looked after them until they hatched. It was so exciting, I couldn't wait for them to hatch.

At last they hatched. It was night-time. I went into my time machine. When I went home I had a cup of tea and had a little snooze and had a little think about where I was going next time.

I really miss Dinosaur Land.

MOHAMMED RAYHAAN PANJWANI (6)
UPLANDS INFANT SCHOOL, LEICESTER

UNTITLED

One snowy day, I found a magical time machine. I sat on the time machine seat...

I looked around myself and I saw dinosaurs stamping in the glimmering pond!

I heard dinosaurs roaring really loudly.

I saw a bright white egg, when I touched it it was starting to hatch.

One really nice dinosaur said, 'Do you want to come with me? I could teach you how to fly.'

Afterwards, I went back to the magical time machine and I went back to my comfy, cosy house. I fell asleep in my bed.

KAREEMA KHALIFA (6)
UPLANDS INFANT SCHOOL, LEICESTER

KASEERA'S DINOSAUR ADVENTURE

One summer's day, I found a shiny time machine. I jumped in the time machine and it took me to Dinosaur Land. I saw a dinosaur roaring to the other dinosaur.

Suddenly, *stomp, stomp!* A massive dinosaur came to me and roared at me. While it was roaring it dropped a colourful, spotty egg. I caught the spotty egg just in time before it cracked. Then I quickly put it safe and sound in my huge bag.

After a while, I could hear a cracking sound from my bag. I opened my bag and I saw the egg hatching.

I felt very excited. Out popped a baby dinosaur. It was so cute and smooth! My time in Dinosaur Land was nearly ending, so I gently picked the baby dinosaur up and put it back in his mummy's nest.

As I was walking by, I saw the mummy dinosaur so happy because I kept her baby dinosaur safe. She flew so fast to her nest to see her new beautiful baby.

After my wild adventure, it was time to go home. I jumped back in the time machine. I pulled the lever and *whoosh!* I got back home, wishing it was all real.

KASEERA KHAN (6)
UPLANDS INFANT SCHOOL, LEICESTER

UNTITLED

One windy day, Percy the dolphin was swimming fast because a shark was after her. Percy was looking for her school to help her. Soon she found her school and was safe.

Then Percy decided to watch the sunset with her school. The sun was going down, it was beautiful because the sun was orange.

It made them feel what it might look like in summer. Soon their mum came and took them home and put them all in bed. And everybody went to sleep and floated through the sea.

And soon a shark gang came and were looking for all the dolphins so they could eat them for tea. They searched for the dolphins until they saw something at the top of the sea, wiggling. They said, 'At last, we've found the dolphins!'

Percy woke up and her friends were gone and the only thing that was there was blood. Percy's school were dead.

Soon a little fish came and said, 'I'm hungry,' so Percy gave it some food and found a new friend.

Zahra Rinde (6)
Uplands Infant School, Leicester

UNTITLED

There is a lion.
The lion comes and scares everyone away.
I came to help with my rope.
I threw the rope and got the lion.
I rode the lion to show the people.
Balloons appeared and I went with the lion into a magic portal/circle.

JAGRUT MOHAN (7)
UPLANDS INFANT SCHOOL, LEICESTER

AMELIA'S JUNGLE STORY

Once in a jungle, a deep, dark jungle, a little Amelia was walking when she met a snake.

The snake was very kind, he led Amelia through the jungle. Amelia found a tent, the tent was made out of sticks, leaves and vines.

Next to the tent was a swing, a very high swing made of sticks and string.

The fierce snake came and ruined it! Amelia and the kind snake ran and ran.

The snake was furious, his name was the Big Bad Snake! He broke the jungle leaves and conkers far and wide.

Amelia and the kind snake met a lion, his name was Lion. At first Lion did not see them. Lion peered through the vines and leapt out of the vines and said hello.

Lion fixed every little bit of the jungle. He followed the snake and Amelia all around the jungle.

Eventually Lion, Snake and Amelia found Amelia's house, they went inside.

AMELIA AYERS (5)
WEEDON BEC PRIMARY SCHOOL, NORTHAMPTON

SIOBHAN'S JUNGLE STORY

There was a deep, dark forest with trees. It was very damp and there were a lot of bushes.
There was a long snake slithering on a branch.
The snake got angry and showed his terrible teeth.
A lion peeked through the bushes.
The lion ran away through the bushes.
Then he went home.

SIOBHAN LAVERY (6)
WEEDON BEC PRIMARY SCHOOL, NORTHAMPTON

LORI'S JUNGLE STORY

Once upon a time, I went to the jungle and I saw a lion and a snake.
The snake was sliding along a tree branch, the snake looked happy.
Later I disturbed the snake when it was sleeping and it woke up and
bit me! I then ran away and it fell back to sleep.
Then the lion got ready to pounce and he landed on the snake's back.
The snake ran away and the lion never saw him again.
Then the lion went home.

LORI JOHNSON (5)
WEEDON BEC PRIMARY SCHOOL, NORTHAMPTON

Laura's Jungle Story

In the jungle there were some trees. The owls were in the jungle.
There was a snake in the tree, the snake was wiggly.
The snake was angry and had sharp teeth.
There was a lion who was cute and funny. He liked looking through the leaves in the jungle.
The lion was running and smiling.
He was on a log and found his house.

Laura Gurney (5)
Weedon Bec Primary School, Northampton

REBECCA'S JUNGLE STORY

There was a dark forest, there were eyes of bats, they were scary. I wondered what they were doing.

I saw a snake, it was very peaceful, I really liked him. He was the best snake ever! He was very nice.

Uh oh, a mean snake! What should I do? He is scary, he will bite me! How can I stop him?

Look, a peaceful lion, I like him. He is playing in the leaves.

The lion pounced out of the leaves. He was running around the forest.

He looked so sweet, he was so sweet. I loved him.

He came to my house.

REBECCA GEORGINA MERREY (6)

WEEDON BEC PRIMARY SCHOOL, NORTHAMPTON

THE END!

YOUNG WRITERS INFORMATION

We hope you have enjoyed reading this book – and that you will continue to in the coming years.

If you're a young writer who enjoys reading and creative writing, or the parent of an enthusiastic poet or story writer, do visit our website www.youngwriters.co.uk. Here you will find free competitions, workshops and games, as well as recommended reads, a poetry glossary and our blog.

If you would like to order further copies of this book, or any of our other titles give us a call or visit www.youngwriters. co.uk.

Young Writers

Remus House

Coltsfoot Drive

Peterborough

PE2 9BF

(01733) 890066 / 898110

info@youngwriters.co.uk